This book is dedicated to all those
who enjoy the beliefs and dreams of their fellow beings.
John Jackson

I'd like to dedicate this book to John Jackson and Claire Alderton,
who, each in their own way, made it possible for me to express myself honestly and freely.
Daniela Jaglenka Terrazzini

First published in Great Britain by
JJ Books in 2013.

Copyright © John Jackson 2013

Illustrations by Daniela Jaglenka Terrazzini

ISBN 978-0-9569212-8-4

Contents

Tales of Creation

The Beginning

The Beginning

In the beginning there was nothing. Nor was there any time. All was space and void. Then the space and the void were filled with sound and the sound was Aum. The sound of Aum filled the whole of the space and the void, and Aum was in everywhere and through everywhere and was everywhere. The sound of Aum became power and the power had form with three faces. They were the faces of the Lords of Creation - Brahma the Creator, Vishnu the Preserver and Shiva the Destroyer.

The faces had minds and the mind of Brahma turned to thoughts of creation and he dreamt of it. Firstly from his mind he dreamt seven wise men. They were the first of creation. They were the children of the mind of Brahma. To the seven wise men he gave wives and to one of them, named Kasyapa, he gave two wives, Diti and Aditi.

All the wise men and their wives made many children but Kasyapa with his two wives Diti and Aditi made the most children of all. All the children of Diti were demons and all the children of Aditi were gods. The children of Diti and Aditi were the first demons and the first gods. The demons were mostly bad, but not all bad; and the gods were mostly good, but not all good. The demons and the gods did not love one another and fought against one another all the time. The king of the gods was named Indra and the king of the demons was named V'ritra.

Then Brahma dreamt the world. He made the earth and the lakes and the rivers. He made air and he made fire. He made the mountains so high that their tops soared into the heavens and became the playground of the gods. He made the oceans so deep that they cooled the nether regions in which the demons were, and which were under the world.

The Lord Brahma made all the living things to fill the world that lay between the gods in the mountaintops and the demons in the underworld. He made the trees and the plants, the fishes and the birds. He made the animals. And he made man. When he made the reptiles, Vasuki the cobra slipped and slithered through a crack in the floor of the world and coiled himself up in a cave under the world. The cave was called Nagaloka and became the home of all the snakes.

The Lord Brahma looked on everything that he had made and smiled.

"It is the beginning of the first world," he said. And time began.

The Curse

Soon after the beginning of the first world, one of the seven wise men born of the mind of Brahma named Durvasas came bearing a gift to the palace of Indra, the King of the Gods. The palace of Indra was high and beautiful and in its first courtyard Indra kept his thunderbolts. The thunderbolts were the weapons Indra used in his fights with V'ritra, the first and driest of the demons. Each time Indra threw his thunderbolts at V'ritra, the sky cracked open and the rains came to quench the thirst of Agni, who was the fire god and the twin brother of Indra.

When Durvasas was at the entrance to Indra's palace he raised his hand and beat upon the great door of the entrance gate.

"Ho, Indra," he called. "Ho, Indra, open this gate and let me enter."

"Who calls me?" answered Indra, with a rumble of thunder. "Who wakes me on this afternoon?"

"It is I," replied Durvasas. "I, Durvasas, your uncle. I bring you a gift."

"Enter," called Indra, "but come no further than my first courtyard."

Durvasas pushed open the great door and entered the first of Indra's courtyards. He was nettled by the shortness of Indra's welcome. He was born from the mind of the Lord Brahma and was used to respect from his nephews, the gods.

"Is not my palace beautiful?" asked Indra, when he came into the courtyard to stand before Durvasas. "Is it not the finest palace in the heavens? What is your gift?"

"I bring you the magic flower of the soma plant," replied Durvasas.

"And what is its magic?" asked Indra.

"Why, Indra," said Durvasas, "everyone in the heavens and in the world and in the nether regions knows that. You may have the finest palace in the heavens but even here will you find that when you put the magic soma flower between your teeth your feet begin to dance."

"Dance?" cried Indra. "Dance? Who would want to dance? We in the heavens have no need for dancing." And, plucking the flower from the hand of Durvasas, he gave a scornful flick of his wrist and sent it sailing across the courtyard towards an elephant that was resting himself in the shade of one of the walls.

The elephant stretched out his trunk, gently picking up the flower and placing it in his mouth. Very soon the elephant began to dance - slowly at first, but then faster and faster. Round and round he turned with spreading ears and trunk raised to the heavens until at last he caught a foot on one of Indra's thunderbolts, tottered off balance and, catching hold of Durvasas to try to save himself, fell with a mighty crash and a great cloud of dust right in the middle of the courtyard.

"Fool!" muttered Indra, and placing his toe under the elephant's middle, gently

raised him to his feet, leaving Durvasas to stand himself up again unaided. Where the elephant had fallen was a hint of fragrance and a small stain spreading on the stones. It was all that was left of the magic flower.

Durvasas was very angry. He was very angry because he had been very frightened, and very frightened in front of someone he had come to impress. Moreover, that someone was his young nephew who had rejected his gift.

"I curse you, Indra!" cried out Durvasas, making himself tall and very straight. "I curse you and all you have, and all your brothers and all they have." Spinning on his heels, he stalked out of Indra's palace and down into the world below, muttering and mumbling as he went.

The Milk Ocean

Soon the curse of Durvasas did its work, and Indra and all his brothers were in great distress. Their strength was failing, their eyes were dim and they were losing their fights with the demons. At length, Varuna, the God of the Oceans, came to the palace of Indra.

"This must be ended," he declared. "We must ask for help from the Lord Brahma."

So, in a great band, the gods dragged themselves wearily to see the Lord Brahma the Creator and the maker of the first world. Brahma took them to the feet of the Lord Vishnu, the Preserver. They told the Lord Vishnu of the curse of Durvasas, the cause of their miseries. Vishnu looked deep inside himself, gave his mind to the matter and decided that only a bowl of ambrosia made from the juice of the soma plant, which bears the magic flowers, could restore their vigour. This could only be found by churning the Milk Ocean.

No ordinary churning stick could move the depths of the Milk Ocean, which stretched to the bottom of the world and half the way across it. The only thing suitable for the purpose was the mountain Mandara. But the gods were too weak to lift a mountain, let alone set it turning in the ocean.

Tales of Creation

"Make a pact with the demons," said Vishnu. "Promise them a share of the ambrosia for a share of your labours."

"But the demons are already stronger than us, Lord," said the gods. "Fed on ambrosia they will become stronger still."

"I am the Preserver," the Lord Vishnu reminded them.

So the gods made a pact with the demons, and together they uprooted the mountain Mandara and slid it over the side of the world into the Milk Ocean. Then, taking Vasuki, the cobra who lived under the world in Nagaloka, they uncoiled him, twisted him round and round the mountain, and set him ready for use to be pulled as a churning rope.

When Vishnu told the gods to take the end of the rope by Vasuki's head, the demons became suspicious and forced their way to that end, pushing the still-weakened gods down to where the cobra's tail was. The Lord Vishnu smiled, for as the churning progressed the hot air that came in blasts from the mouth of Vasuki would exhaust the demons, while the gods would gain in strength, cooled by the breezes which blew from the surface of the ocean.

After a time Mandara sank into the slime at the bottom of the ocean, and all the straining of the gods and demons on the serpent rope would not make the mountain twirl around.

"Wait," said Vishnu, and changing his shape into that of a turtle, he dived into the ocean and rested the mountain on his back. With the base of the mountain now eased, the churning went faster and faster as the gods and the demons pulled back and forth on the head and tail ends of Vasuki. Soon the ocean began to thicken and solid things came to the surface.

Tales of Creation

First came the moon. High out of the Milk Ocean he rose and hung in the heavens to cast his cold light on the whole world below. Then came a thousand, and more than a thousand, beautiful girls who danced and laughed their starry way across the sky to Indra's palace. Then came the Golden Tree, then the Sacred Cow, and then a giant elephant gleaming white and with four tasks that Indra sent to join his other elephants.

Then came a milk white horse. V'ritra, the King of Demons, sought to bridle the horse but Indra wrested it from him and sent it trotting with flowing mane into the heavens to stand beside the moon.

Faster and faster still the gods and demons turned Mandara in the Milk Ocean with more and more precious things coming to the surface, until there rose from the creamy depths a woman of such wondrous form and beauty that the gods and demons lost their breath from gazing on her and stopped their churning.

"You are Lakshmi, the Spirit of the Earth," said the Lord Vishnu, calling out to claim her. And the beautiful woman joined the Lord Vishnu as his wife.

Again the gods and demons pulled on Vasuki, and this time a mist of blue poison curled from the surface of the ocean and started to creep into the heavens and the world and the underworld and everywhere.

"We are choking!" cried the gods. But Vishnu called on the Lord Shiva the Destroyer, who leaned down and with a deep and mighty breath drew up all the blue mist and held it in his throat.

At last came a fine gold bowl filled with the fragrant ambrosia, carried by an old man who was the first great physician. On seeing him the demons cried out, "Enough of this pact, the gods have taken everything, the ambrosia must be ours!" Letting go of the head of Vasuki they prepared to steal the physician and his bowl and return with their spoils to the underworld. Indra and the gods, now finally tired to such a state that they could only lie on the ground and gasp, cried out to the Lord Vishnu who, taking the form of a beautiful girl, came down again to help them.

In truth, Vishnu had not wished the demons to share the ambrosia when he told the gods to make the pact and he did not wish them to share it now.

"I will serve out the ambrosia," said the Lord Vishnu. The demons were so dazzled by the light coming from the beautiful girl whose form he had taken that they were blinded, and did not see that the ambrosia was served only to the gods and that none was given to them.

But one demon, Rahu, did see this and, more cunning than the rest, placed himself unnoticed amongst the gods. Rahu was just on the point of taking a great gulp from the precious bowl when he was seen by the sun and the moon.

"Stop, thief!" they cried, and Vishnu sent a discus scything through the sky, which struck Rahu and took his head from his shoulders, sending it spinning into the heavens.

When Indra and all the gods had drunk the ambrosia they all grew strong again and returned to their heavens. The demons untwined Vasuki, heaved the mountain Mandara back into place, and with aching arms and sore backs crowded again into the bowels of the earth and the depths of the great salt waters. The Lord Shiva, seeing Vasuki slither slowly on his way back to Nagaloka, bent down, picked him from the rocks and knotted the tired snake at his waist as a girdle.

In this way, the beginning of the first world was finished.

The Lie

This is the story of Kadru, which happened when the first world was new and sparkling and there were no lies.

Kadru came up into the world from Nagaloka to become the mother of all snakes. There she laid a huge egg and brooded it. For five hundred years Kadru lay coiled about her egg, humming to the babies within. One day in the five hundred and first year the egg's outer shell tore like paper, and Kadru's snake-children appeared in their thousands.

When Kadru's children were born, she again felt the glow of youth. As she watched them slipping over the stones and through the pools, and as she heard the leaves and grasses whisper at their passage, she stretched her coils in the sun and laughed with all the pleasure of motherhood.

"Oh, Vinata," she said to her sister who had come to visit her. "Oh, Vinata, how blessed I am in my beautiful children."

"You are blessed indeed, Kadru," said Vinata, and she shifted her golden head to keep a better watch on her nephews and nieces.

Kadru would have liked Vinata to show more admiration. Kadru was pleased with herself and thought that her sister – who had yet to lay a single egg, let alone hatch it into a thousand, and more than a thousand, glistening babies – should show a little more of something – well, yes – admiration. As she lay in the sun, this itch of annoyance grew like a cancer in Kadru's mind.

Presently, a milk white horse came trotting, high tailed and with flowing mane, down from out of the sky.

"Why," said Kadru, turning to Vinata, "it's the horse that came instead of butter when the gods churned the Milk Ocean."

"I know," said Vinata.

"But I am certain you don't know the colour of its tail," said Kadru, who was annoyed that Vinata should know anything at all.

"Do you?" asked Vinata.

"Why, yes," said Kadru. "It's the purest black."

"Oh no, Kadru," said Vinata, laughing. "The hairs in the tail of the horse from the Milk Ocean can only be white."

"Do you argue with me?" demanded Kadru, rearing up with her snake's hood spreading, and ruby fires in her beautiful eyes.

"Not argue, sister," said Vinata. "I just think you are wrong."

"A challenge, then," hissed Kadru in anger. "The one of us who is wrong shall be the slave of the other for one thousand years." Vinata lowered her head in agreement. But she was sad. She loved her sister and took no pleasure in knowing that she,

Vinata, would be proved right.

That night Kadru left her children and crept out to where the horse was grazing in the moonlight. The horse's tail gleamed white as the ocean from whence it came. There was not a black hair in it.

"Vinata's slave – and for a thousand years. Never!" Kadru said to herself, and quickly slithered over the rocks to where her children slept knotted together in a restless black ball of quicksilver.

"Children," she called softly. "Children, come to me, come quickly." Very soon the little snakes lay round Kadru in their thousands, watching her with gleaming eyes.

"Listen, children, and as you value your mother's pride, do as I ask you." So, telling them of her argument with Vinata, she bade them to climb into the horse's tail and, taking hold of its root, hang there in such numbers that it would look black.

Kadru's children looked at her in amazement. Speaking all together they said,

"No mother, we cannot. We must not turn ourselves into a lie."

"Cannot? You will not do it?" cried Kadru. "You are my children. I made you. You must do as I say!"

But the little snakes only writhed around their mother in unhappy confusion and made no move towards the horse's tail.

"Do you dare to disobey me?" screamed Kadru in a fury. She began to dance, coil turning upon coil, urging her children to do her bidding. Her children would not move. Her voice rose to a hissing shriek and, hideous in her anger, she rose and swayed above them with spreading hood and flickering tongue.

The Lie

"Children, the world will despise you for disobeying your mother! You will be feared as unnatural monsters. At the sight of you men will raise their heels to crush you. You will…". Kadru paused, and as she gathered her breath, the sky became a mirror before her and she saw what she had done. She saw the horror of her own reflection. Remorse came to her, but it was too late. She heard the murmur of a million wings as the gods breathed down on her.

"Oh, Kadru, you asked your lovely children to turn themselves into a lie and now, for them, your own words will be the truth."

"But they did not do it," pleaded Kadru.

"Your wish was enough," the gods replied.

So all of Kadru's children, and all snakes that came into the world after them, learnt to lie hidden in the ground and under the roots of trees, far from the fear and heels of men.

The Sons of King Sagara

The Sons of King Sagara

There was in the first world a ruler of a country named Ayodha and his name was Sagara. Sagara was sad. His people were prosperous, the gardens of his palace were filled with the rarest of trees and plants, and dragonflies rustled through the air as he walked beside his fish-filled pools. His two wives, Kerini and Sumati, were beautiful, his kitchens produced the finest foods, and he had everything a ruler could wish for. All, that is, except the one thing he wanted most: children. Finally, Sagara went to consult Bhrigu, one of the seven wise men born of the mind of Brahma.

"What can I do for you?" asked Bhrigu, when Sagara approached him.

"You can help me to have sons," said Sagara.

"Just sons, no daughters?" asked Bhrigu.

"Sons first, then daughters," replied Sagara.

"And how many?" asked Bhrigu.

"As many as my wives will bear me," said Sagara.

"That could be very many," laughed Bhrigu. "Return to your palace, fill your mind with thoughts of sons and your wishes will be granted."

So Sagara returned to his palace, uncertain of Bhrigu's meaning. As he passed through the palace gardens his eyes fell upon a melon vine with its pale green fruit lying cool and luscious on the ground.

"Perhaps I will have as many sons as those melons have seeds," he said to himself. Bhrigu heard the thoughts of Sagara as they were carried on the evening breeze and he chuckled.

In due time Kerini and Sumati swelled with child and on the same evening gave birth. Kerini produced a fine healthy son, but Sumati produced a large ripe melon that fell to the ground and burst open, yielding sixty thousand sons.

"Sixty thousand sons!" said Sagara with pride, quite overlooking the child of Kerini. So busy was he overseeing the raising of the sixty thousand that he gave no thought to their brother. Nor did he give any thought to daughters and neither did Kerini nor Sumati produce any for him.

As Sagara's sons grew so did his pride, until so proud was he that his mind turned to thoughts of a larger and loftier palace. Each morning and each evening as he met with his growing sons this idea grew in him.

"The finest palace ever built...," he thought to himself, and again he went to see Bhrigu.

"And what is it this time?" asked the sage.

"I seek the finest palace ever built," replied Sagara.

"In heaven or on earth?" asked Bhrigu.

The Sons of King Sagara

"The finest anywhere," replied Sagara.

"That is the palace of Indra in the heavens," said Bhrigu, "but to take it you must first throw Indra from his kingdom."

"With sixty thousand sons I can conquer any kingdom," smiled Sagara.

"Maybe," said Bhrigu, "but Indra's kingdom can be taken from him only in one way."

"And what way is that?" asked Sagara.

"You must take your finest white stallion and plait his mane with gold and scarlet thread," said Bhrigu. "Then you must set it loose and follow it with your army of sons. When you have made one hundred conquests, then may you tilt at Indra and push him from his kingdom."

"One hundred conquests to secure the finest palace!" exclaimed Sagara.

"It is your wish, not mine," said Bhrigu.

So Sagara went with his sons to the palace stables. They took out his finest white stallion, put plaits of gold and scarlet in his mane, sent him cantering from the stable yard and prepared to follow him into the world beyond.

But unbeknownst to Sagara, Indra had heard what Bhrigu had said. As soon as the horse was out of sight of the palace walls, Indra disguised himself in the form of a demon and came down from the heavens. Catching the horse by the tail, he pulled it neighing and kicking deep down into the nether regions where he tethered it to the fiery cauldron called Kapila that boils and bubbles in the centre of the earth.

"Now what will you do?" asked Bhrigu with some amusement. The wise man had come to the palace gates to watch Sagara and his army of sons set out in their pursuit of conquest. "There is no kingdom that I know of so near the centre of the earth. You had best get that horse back."

"I will set my sons to dig," said Sagara, and he called for sixty thousand shovels to be made in the royal smithies so that his sons could dig towards the centre of the earth and find the white stallion.

With mighty force and energy did Sagara's sons set about their task. In no time great mounds of rock and sand rose high on the landscape as they scraped and chiselled, tunnelled and burrowed. Each son set himself the task of digging one mile into the earth's depths. But as they dug so the ravished earth cried out for help to Lakshmi, the spirit of the earth and wife of Vishnu, as she lay in the billows of the ocean.

Lakshmi heard the earth's cry and called up to Vishnu, Lord of Creation and The Preserver. Just as the first of Sagara's sons burst into the very centre of the earth, so Vishnu put out his toe and tipped the cauldron called Kapila so that a scalding flood of fire poured into the tunnel, burning all the sons of Sagara to ashes.

When Sagara saw flames and smoke billowing from the centre of the earth, swirling round the piles of excavated rock left by his sons, he knew that some great disaster had overtaken them. Sadly he thought back on all that had happened since he had wished for children.

"And now I fear not one is left," he sighed. Bhrigu heard this and came to comfort Sagara.

"Let your grandson ask the Lord Vishnu what has become of his uncles," he advised.

"Grandson, what grandson have I?" asked Sagara.

Tales of Creation

"He is the boy Ansuman, of the line of Kerini."

In truth, until that moment Sagara had forgotten all about the son born to Kerini, and did not know he had taken a wife. Indeed, he had never before heard of his grandchild Ansuman.

So Sagara summoned Ansuman and told him to seek out Vishnu and ask him the meaning of that great belch of flame, and Ansuman set out on his quest. He had gone some way from his grandfather's palace and was on the point of looking for a path to the heavens when Garuda, the half-man, half-eagle messenger of Vishnu, flew down to him.

"First find the cauldron called Kapila, a thousand miles below you," Garuda croaked.

Ansuman began to search for a place in the earth where he could creep down through the nether regions, down to the very centre of the earth and find the roaring, reeking cauldron Kapila.

Down and down went Ansuman, past Nagaloka the cavern filled with hissing snakes; past the pit of slime and ooze which held the buffalo demon Mehisha; past the jewel-encrusted palace of V'ritra, King of the Demons; past the endless graves, the home of the Pisachas which come like goblins to eat the flesh of the dead; past the silent lakes filled by the clouds stolen by the black and creeping Dasyus; past the home of the Vartikas which have one wing, one eye, one leg and vomit blood; and finally between the legs of the giant elephants holding the earth on their backs, and into the vaulted cavern holding the cauldron Kapila.

And there, still tethered and still with his plaited mane, was the white stallion from his grandfather's palace stables. Quietly and carefully, with half an eye on that fearsome bubbling pot, Ansuman untied the horse. Looking around him it was clear what had become of his uncles. In one corner of the cavern was the entrance to a tunnel, and as far back as Ansuman could see the tunnel was clogged with char and ashes all mixed with twisted, half-melted shovel blades, arm bangles and sandal buckles.

"Oh, my poor uncles," thought Ansuman. Quietly leading the horse he crept out of the cavern, between the legs of the giant elephants, up through all the horrors and terrors of the nether regions and into the world again.

"Well, I see you found it," said a voice. It was the messenger Garuda who had flown down from the peaks of the mountains again to greet Ansuman on his return.

"Did you also find your uncles?"

"They are nothing but ashes," replied Ansuman. "The tunnel they dug is filled with them. Now what should I do?"

"Go back to your grandfather," said Garuda. "Return his stallion to him and tell him that he must pray to the Lord Vishnu for the river of the goddess Ganga to come down to earth. Then will his sons be restored to life." The mighty Garuda flapped his wings and soared once again into the heavens.

So Ansuman led the white stallion back to the palace of his grandfather and told Sagara of everything he had seen and of everything Garuda had said.

Now at that time the river Ganges ran in the heavens only, amongst the gods. The spirit of the river was the goddess Ganga. She was loved greatly by all the gods and was smiled upon especially by Lord Vishnu the Preserver. The source of the river was the toe of Vishnu and, gaining in size and strength, it ran pure and clear in rills and rapids tumbling down and round and through the kingdoms of the gods. As it ran it filled the air with the sound of Ganga's laughing, chuckling music.

When the first of Sagara's prayers reached Vishnu, he said,

"Ask the Lord Brahma. If it is his wish then will I shake the goddess Ganga loose from my toe." And so again Sagara prayed, this time to the Lord Brahma.

"Prayers for one hundred years may move me to let the goddess Ganga loose, but you must pray to the Lord Shiva also," was the reply, and so again Sagara prayed, now to the Lord Shiva.

"And what is this to do with me?" Shiva asked of Brahma and Vishnu. "The sons of Sagara are ashes already. They are no concern of mine."

"You," said Brahma, "must break the fall of the goddess Ganga on her way to earth in case her weight should sweep the world away and there would be nothing left of it."

So as he was told, Sagara prayed to the Lord Brahma night and morning for the rest of his life. At his death he gave his kingdom to his brave young grandson Ansuman and told him to pray to the Lord Brahma also. On his death Ansuman passed the task together with the Kingdom of Ayodhu to his son Dilipa, who in turn passed both kingdom and task to his son Bhagiratha. And Bhagiratha, knowing that the one hundred years decreed by Brahma would be completed in his lifetime, added his prayers to Shiva also.

When the one hundred years were completed Brahma nodded to Vishnu, who with a gentle flick of his foot shook Ganga from his toe. As she fell, Ganga turned from a pleasant rippling brook into a roaring foaming flood that poured down the peak of Kailas towards the earth. The Lord Shiva heard Ganga coming carrying earth and rocks and sand in a slurry of brown mud and, in answer to the prayers of Bhagiratha, Dilipa, Ansuman and Sagara, stood up and braced himself so that the torrential river flowed through the filter of his hair and fell to earth in seven even streams.

Bhagiratha called out to his people to dig a channel so that water from one of the seven streams could flow into the tunnel dug by the sons of Sagara so many years before. The water oozed and trickled down and down until it reached the very centre of the earth. The fire in the cauldron Kapila turned this water into steam, so that a mighty blast blew the ashy remains of the sons of Sagara up through the tunnel as a thick grey plume that reached to the very top of the mountains in the heavens. There it settled in a fine layer of dust that spread over all the kingdoms of the gods, where it remained until the end of time.

In that way were the sons of Sagara brought to life again. And the river of the goddess Ganga stayed to flow on earth.

The Fish

Near to the end of the first world and before the beginning of this world Manu, a healer and teacher who knew many things, and who had an old and bright soul that had lived many lives, was standing on the banks of the river named Saraswati searching his mind so as to be near the maker of all things. Suddenly a fish leapt from the water and flopped about on the shore with a fat belly, bulging eyes and a great thick-lipped, gasping mouth.

"Master," said the fish, "Master, save me from the monster in this stream who would devour me."

"Certainly," said Manu, and he took the fish and placed it in an earthenware jar.

The days passed and the fish grew and grew. It grew so fast and so big that soon Manu had no choice but to break the jar and place the fish in a pond.

In no time at all the fish had grown too large for the pond. So large, in fact, that it could not keep its scaly back under the water.

"Master," said the fish, "Master, save me from the sun which is scorching my back. Take me to the River Ganges."

"Certainly," said Manu. Taking a wet sack, he wrapped the fish in it and carried the great creature on his shoulders to the banks of the Ganges.

But in the River Ganges, the same thing happened. The fish grew. It grew so large that its fins lay on either bank. It blocked the water channels so that the river rose up, flooding fields and cities for a hundred miles around.

"Take me to the ocean," said the fish.

"Certainly," said Manu. So Manu and the fish set off for the ocean, the fish swimming down the Ganges, Manu walking along the bank beside him. Finally they reached the great eastern sea and the fish, turning in the rolling surf that beat upon the golden sands, smiled at Manu and said,

"Manu, now look at me and see. I am Brahma, I am the self-existing, and I am the framer and creator of all things."

"Yes, Lord," said Manu. "What do you wish of me, Lord?" For Manu knew that if Brahma had lived with him all this time, it was for some great purpose.

"Manu," said Brahma, "this world will soon be ended by a great deluge and all will perish. But so that there may be wisdom and life in the next world, build me a broad boat and furnish it with a long rope, and place in it the seven wise men born of my mind and all the seeds of life and knowledge."

"Yes, Lord," said Manu.

"And when you are ready with the boat the floods will come and I will return to you so that together we may find the next world." And so speaking, the great fish sank from view beneath the waves, leaving Manu alone and lonely on the silent shore.

The Fish

So Manu collected together all the pieces of wood the eastern sea threw up and made them into a great boat. He pulled the leaves from the high palms and wove their fibres into sails, and he cut the grasses growing by the seashore and plaited them into a long rope. He called to him the seven wise men born of the mind of Brahma and bade them bring together and store in the bowels of the boat all the seeds of life and knowledge.

The waters came and the sea rose and the gales pushed Manu and his boat far off into the grey and foam-flecked waves. Then Brahma in the form of a fish rose up from out of the depths and called Manu to him. Manu fastened the rope to the two golden horns that sprouted from the fish's head.

"Take down your sails," the fish called up to Manu. "Take down your sails and I will pull you for a thousand years until we find the peak of Himavan."

And the rain fell until the mountains and the forests vanished. The waters rose still further until they touched the sky, and there was no more land to be seen and the entire world was water. Nothing in that world, nor in the heavens, nor in the underworld could stay alive. But the fish pulled slowly and surely, and Manu and the seven wise men that had collected all the seeds of life and knowledge moved safely into the winds and currents and across the new grey depths.

Finally they reached the one peak that stayed above the watery waste.

"This is Himavan," the fish called up. "Here, Manu, you must wait until the seas go down."

And in another thousand years the waters dropped and took Manu with them. In time he and his boat and all within it were set down on a great plain. The fish unleashed the boat and swam off in the last of the water.

"Build this new world well and set your seeds to sprout," the fish called back to Manu.

Soon all the creatures that had been in the first world, the birds and fishes, people and animals, and all the wondrous trees and flowers and grasses, were born again and lived between the gods in the heavens and the demons in the nether regions. Manu went again to stand and think on the banks of the river Saraswati. And Brahma, pleased with all that had passed, took the goddess of that river as his wife and named her, in her turn, Saraswati.

That was how Manu came to make the beginning of the second world and how Saraswati joined Brahma, the Lord of Creation, as his wife and became the spirit of learning.

Tales of Destruction

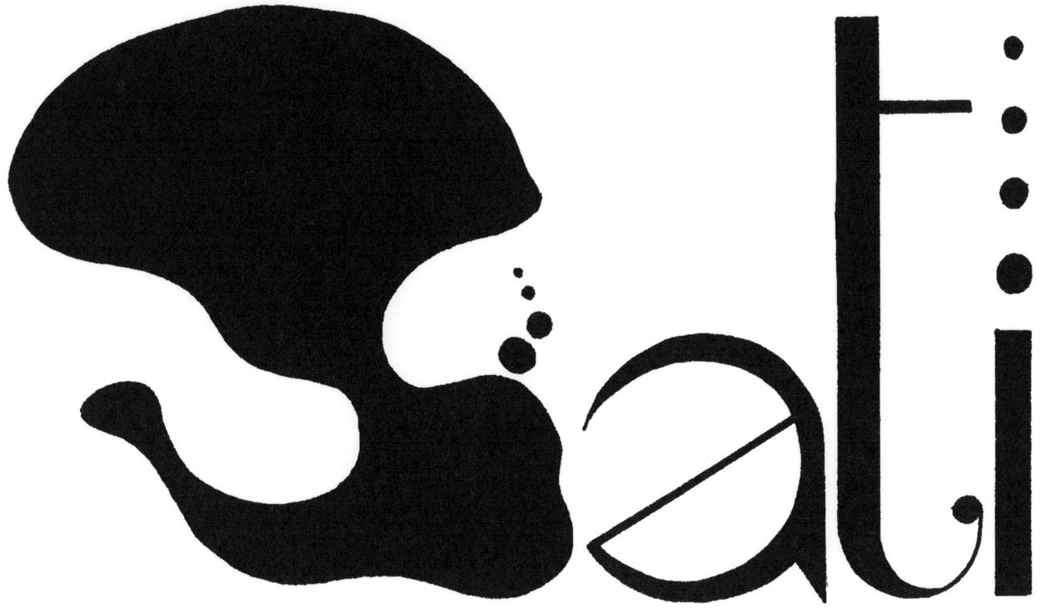

Sati

Now, of Brahma, Vishnu and Shiva, only Shiva was without a wife. This worried Shiva greatly. As he watched Brahma glide across the heavens on his great white swan with Saraswati at his side and Vishnu sport with the milky Lakshmi in the billows of the ocean, he asked himself, "And why not me?"

The truth was that in the eyes of many, Shiva lacked grace. Nor was he handsome. Fearsome and regal he was, but not handsome. A slit in the middle of his forehead concealed his third eye, which scorched all it ever looked on. His hair hung down in matted strands and the smell of burning bodies was on his breath. For clothes he wore the skin of a tiger, with Vasuki, that long and scaly cobra, knotted at his waist as a belt. Round his neck he wore a necklace of charred skulls which scarce concealed the blue mark carried from the time he swallowed down the poison fog that came from the milk ocean. To make matters worse Shiva, consumed in thought, would wander through the heavens and through the world muttering, "And why not me?" without noticing whom and what he passed. It was in such a way that Shiva came to pass the palace of Daksha, one of the seven wise men born of the mind of Brahma.

Tales of Destruction

Daksha and his wife Prasuti had spent their lives making daughters. Now all their daughters but one had married. That one was Sati, their youngest daughter. Sati was unmarried and would look at neither god nor man - not that Daksha would have welcomed a man. All his daughters had married gods, sons of Kasyapa and Aditi, and he took pride in this, as he did in his power and his wealth and the glory of his palace. Sadly, he took no pride in Sati. The girl angered him with her simple clothes and quietly downcast looks. He felt she brought no honour to his house.

"Too meek. Too meek and too mouse-like," he grumbled to Prasuti. "We must find her a godly husband."

"Patience, husband," counselled Prasuti.

It so happened that Sati was with Daksha outside the palace wall, watching a green lizard that he had summoned her to see, when Shiva came shambling by.

"Rude fellow," Daksha complained as the Lord of Creation passed them by, with no sign that he had seen Sati or her father. "A very rude fellow, and he reeks of death."

"Oh, father," said Sati, "he is so beautiful."

"Beautiful! He is a disgrace to creation and all that is in it." And so saying, Daksha stomped off, swishing at the flower heads and working himself up into a fine temper. But Sati had seen into the soul and nature of Shiva and she understood that his need to destroy was born of duty and of beauty.

"Shiva needs to destroy so that the Lord Brahma can create again, and the worlds can go on and on for ever," she murmured happily to herself as she followed her father back to the palace, picking up the bruised flowers and placing them in her hair and

behind her ears. Delighting in the joy of truth she returned to her chambers declaring, "Shiva, you are so beautiful!" to herself over and over again. The Lord Shiva heard her and his heart leapt. Daksha heard her also.

"We must finish this!" he said to Prasuti. "Sati must choose a husband. Summon all the unmarried gods."

So all the unmarried gods came to Daksha's palace and Sati, obedient to her father's wish, came down into the finest room of the palace, the great hall, dressed as a bride. As was the custom, she carried a garland of fragrant fresh flowers picked from the palace gardens.

Richly and handsomely attired, the gods stood waiting upon Daksha and his daughter. Daksha swelled with pride to know that they had come at his bidding to be chosen by his daughter. To the feelings of Sati he gave not a thought.

"Choose, daughter," he whispered in her ear, "choose."

"But father," said Sati, with growing dismay, "father, where is the Lord Shiva? He is unmarried and he is a Lord of Creation. He is even more than a god."

"Shiva!" raged Daksha, his face purpling, "Shiva! Do you think I would invite that vagabond, that mean-faced, grimy mutterer? I struck him from the list. Choose, daughter, and do not shame your father."

But Sati set her mouth and shook her head. "No, father, I will obey you in everything but this. Call Shiva."

"By the sword of Indra I will not," cried Daksha in a rage. "Call Shiva? Never!"

"Then I will," said Sati quietly, "and none here will I marry."

Sati

With those words she cast her garland high towards the heavens, calling, "Shiva, come to me! Oh, my beautiful Shiva, it is you that I choose."

And then a wondrous thing happened. Before the eyes of Daksha and Prasuti and all that mighty company of gods came the answer to her call. Shiva himself stood before them, and around his neck was the garland that Sati had thrown to the heavens.

The other gods left Daksha's palace in a stream of golden chariots, and Sati and Shiva too prepared to leave.

"Your father has not blessed you," said Shiva.

"He is hurt now, but he will in time," replied Sati.

"And we must walk, I have no chariot," continued her new husband.

"No matter, we have each other," said Sati.

And, with great love in her heart, she took the Lord Shiva's hand and started the long walk to his home on the peak of Kailas, a place wreathed in clouds of silence and set high in the snowy mountains.

Burning love

Burning Love

S ome time after Sati and Shiva had settled down to make their home in the ice and snow of Kailas, they had a visitor. Sati had seen no one since she had left her own home and so any visitor was very welcome. This visitor was the sage Narada. Narada was another of the seven wise men born of the mind of Brahma. He was more clever than he was wise, and he sang with a fine voice, but, like many clever men, he was also a great mischief.

Sitting on the peak of Kailas, Shiva saw Narada coming. "Hmmm - a trouble maker," he thought to himself as he stood up from his rocky seat and went to see why Narada had come. Narada seemed to have come for nothing in particular, and he chatted away about this and that; how the thrushes were remarkably songful this year, and how fine Indra's new elephant was, and all manner of things.

"Of course, you'll hear all about this at the banquet," Narada said suddenly, putting his head on one side and looking at Sati with bird-bright eyes.

"Banquet?" asked Sati.

"Why, Daksha's, of course," said Narada. "The whole of Heaven is coming. With all those daughters, and all those gods they married, even Daksha's palace will hardly have room to hold them! Hasn't your invitation come yet?" he enquired with another bird-like look.

"Not yet," said Sati, flushing a little.

"Nor will it," added Shiva, grimly.

"I'm sure it will," she replied.

"Of course it will," said Narada. "You do live far away, but what father giving a banquet would forget his youngest daughter and her husband?" And so saying, Narada set off down the mountain again, skipping and chuckling as he went.

"One day he will learn what the monkeys have learnt," remarked Shiva as he watched Narada go.

"What do you mean, husband?" asked Sati.

"That if you make sparks with stones in the forest, you may set fire to your own tail," replied Shiva.

For some days neither Sati nor Shiva made mention of Narada's visit.

"I'm sure father has forgiven me by now," said Sati quietly to herself.

"A daughter should not need an invitation to her father's house – nor should her husband," said Shiva to himself. But no invitation came.

At last, Sati's patience cracked. She missed her home and her mother, Prasuti; she missed her sisters and their husbands. She even missed her father, Daksha, for all his bad temper.

"He did show me that green lizard," she thought to herself.

Burning Love

"Shiva," she said, "Lord Shiva, my beloved husband, even though my father has not invited us - "

The Lord Shiva cut her short. "No. It would not be right for you to go. Your father has not blessed us."

"Oh husband, please," said Sati, "for my mother's sake!"

"No." said Shiva. "Once and for all. No."

And so she pleaded, and pleaded, and pleaded, until at last Shiva gave way. Sati walked down from the mountains with lightness in her step, but Shiva returned slowly to his rock on the peak of Kaila with heaviness in his.

After many days' travel Sati, dressed in homespun cloth with wild flowers in her hair and simple sandals on her feet, arrived at last at her father's palace. The roads leading to it were filled with the horse-drawn chariots that had brought the guests. The sound of music filled the air and a great mound of fire shone into the sky and lit the countryside for miles around. Shyly, Sati entered the great hall where last she had stood briefly as a bride. Seated at the far end was her father, receiving the line of guests in their gorgeous costumes. Near to him sat her mother. Sati looked with love upon them both.

"Oh, mother!" she cried, running towards her. Past all the guests she ran, not noticing the sly smiles and sniggering mouths and lifted eyebrows.

"Stop!" cried the angry voice of Daksha.

"Stop! Do you dare approach your mother? Do you dare come into this, my house that you shamed so wantonly?"

"Please, father." said Sati "Please." And she stood shocked by the bile in her father's voice.

"Please?" cried her father. "Please? And whom did you please when you left your father's house to live with that vile creature, that lover of skulls?"

"He is my beloved husband, father," pleaded Sati, looking at her mother and her sisters and their husbands and all the other guests. But they all looked away from her.

"And how does this husband dress you?" continued Daksha, following Sati as she recoiled from him with her face in her hands. "Were these fine clothes stripped from a corpse before its burning?" Daksha took a staff from a palace guard and twitched at Sati's clothing in disdain. Sati fled from this terrible onslaught of hate and ridicule into the courtyard, where the ceremonial fire burned.

"Cringing little creature," called Daksha after her. "Is this what the husband you find so beautiful has brought you to? Beautiful! He has the beauty of this spittle I send after you – pray take it to him, it is my wedding gift." So saying, Daksha spat a great gob onto the marble floor and turning his back to Sati stalked back into the hall.

"Father!" screamed Sati, with the agony of hurt and shame. "You have rejected me and Shiva, whom I love, with me – by this I will shield him from your hatred." As she spoke she turned towards the fire and on her final words flung herself into the flames.

"Stop her!" cried Prasuti, but it was too late. In horror and terror Daksha and Prasuti rushed to the fire as the flames rose higher and higher, consuming poor Sati. But the flames took only Sati's life. Her body, clothed in its simple robe with her wild flowers and rush sandals, remained untouched and she lay on the fiery bed of flames as if sleeping.

When the winds brought Shiva the news of Sati's death and the manner of it, he gave out a great curse.

"Though I hate the demons, now will I call upon them to help me! I will call as many demons as there are hairs on my head to help me murder Daksha!" And as he cursed, the earth cracked open and demons hissing fire burst from the underworld and raced towards the palace of Daksha, with V'ritra at their head. More and more they came until they merged into a thick bubbling river of flame. Shiva called out to his bride.

"Sati, I come to avenge you!" And he strode with great steps through the sky, until he stood outside the entrance to Daksha's palace.

With his third eye opened Shiva burned down the wooden gates and, with V'ritra and his demons close on his heels, stormed in. Daksha, now a cowardly man mourning his daughter's tragic death, had taken refuge behind Prasuti as Shiva burst in. With a great bound Shiva leaped high into the air and, reaching behind Prasuti, caught Daksha by the hair on the top of his head. For one moment he held Daksha kicking high above the floor, before V'ritra, with one blow of his demon's sword, took off his head.

"Please, Lord!" cried Prasuti, kneeling beside the body of Daksha which lay with blood gushing from its headless neck. Shiva paused, for he remembered that this was Sati's mother, whom she had loved so much. Taking V'ritra's sword he struck off the head of a goat and fixed it on to where Daksha's head had been.

"Mother," he said, "now take your goat-headed husband and join your daughters before this palace is consumed by flames."

Then Shiva lifted the corpse of Sati from the pyre and draped it across his shoulders, leaving V'ritra and the demons to carry out their reckless burning of the palace. Into

Burning Love

the plains and into the valleys went Shiva with his burden, and as he passed, the world began to die. The lakes and rivers dried. The clouds would yield no rain. The corn withered in the fields and the night skies were lit and ruddy as the forests burned.

The gods were shocked. They had seen the molten torrent of demons engulf the palace where lately they had feasted with their wives. They had seen Daksha run goat-headed from the piles of smoking ash, where now everything was scorched in the flames of Shiva's grief. So they went to Lord Vishnu the Preserver and cried to him for help. When Vishnu heard their cries, he took his bow and began to shoot arrows towards the earth. Each arrow that flew took a piece from Sati's body as it lay across Shiva's shoulders. The pieces fell upon the ground and where each piece fell, a spring of water came, a small oasis in a thirsty land. Fifty-two arrows sped from Vishnu's bow and fifty-two times a spring appeared. When all his arrows were spent, Vishnu returned to Lakshmi and his ocean to rest.

Lightened of Sati's body, Shiva continued sadly home to Kailas. He sat, looking deep inside himself and pondering everything that had come to pass.

"But why?" he asked, "why did this happen to me?" As he pondered, silence and a great cold came upon the world and on the heavens and on the underworld. And the head of the demon Rahu caught the sun in its mouth so that there was no light. The stars and the moon stopped shining, and even time stood still.

Taraka

The great cold that was brought upon the world and on the heavens and on the underworld by Shiva's grief came to the notice of Taraka, a powerful demon.

"The gods are losing power," he said to himself. "Now is the time to avenge the churning of the Milk Ocean."

The demons had never forgotten nor forgiven the way they had been tricked into labouring to produce riches and power for the gods.

Takara set himself deep in the ocean, and with serpents coiling round his feet he dreamt a spell to summon Brahma, the Lord of Creation. Deeply he dreamt, until great rounded bubbles carrying his spell rose from the depths and burst upon the surface of the ocean, releasing their summons. On hearing it Brahma mounted his swan and seared across the heavens in a burst of white light, gliding down into the world and settling on the water.

"Who calls me?" asked Brahma, peering down into the green and grey depths from the back of his swan. "Who summons me?"

"It is I," answered Taraka and he rose from the ocean floor in a string of bubbles.

"And what is it that you want?" asked Brahma of the weed-encrusted demon now spinning and bobbing in the waves beside him.

"I want you to grant me one wish," said Taraka.

"And what is that?" asked Brahma.

"I wish," replied the demon, "I wish that my life can be ended by one hand only."

"And whose hand is that?" asked Brahma.

"The hand of a son of Shiva," announced Taraka.

"That wish I certainly grant you," said Brahma, and urging his steed into a slow and powerful flight he left the waters of the world and sped upwards through the stars that danced round Indra's palace.

When the gods heard of the wish Brahma had granted Taraka they were dismayed.

"But Brahma, Lord Brahma," they cried, "Shiva is wrapped in grief and the body of Sati, his wife, is scattered by the arrows of Vishnu; how then will a son of Shiva come to save us from Taraka?"

Brahma looked down on the gods, and then across to where Shiva sat frozen and unmoving on the peak of Kailas, and he said nothing.

"Now we are lost indeed," cried the gods in fear and misery.

"Now they are lost indeed," cried Taraka, sure that he had tricked Brahma into granting him immortality. And gathering a multitude of demons, many of whom had been at the sacking of Daksha's palace, Taraka leapt into his fiery chariot, lashing the

serpents that pulled it into a frenzy and careered towards the kingdom of the gods.

Great was the havoc as the demon horde drove all before them. They smashed down the gates of Indra's palace and cut off the tusks of his elephants. They rode out to Indra's stables beside the moon and took the milk white horse that was in the finest of them. They smeared paste in the sky so that the moon, the home of Chandra the Moon God, became fixed, shining full and could neither wax nor wane. They found the palace of Kubera, the God of Wealth, and pillaged his treasure vaults. They shot arrows at the sun so that they pricked Surya the Sun God, and then they chased the maidens who were the stars. They stripped the fruit from the Golden Tree. They seized Vayu, the God of Winds, and taking him by his streaming hair whirled him round and round so that storms and tempests went screaming through the skies. They stole the blushes from the cheeks of Ushas, the Dawn Goddess. They stuffed rocks into the mouth of the goddess Ganga. They locked Yama the God of Death in his southern dungeons. They put ice into the ears of Agni the Fire God so that water came from his mouth instead of flames and they stole everything they could see. Finally, as they streamed, loot laden, back towards the underworld, they surged into the fields of the seven wise men and stole the Sacred Cow that had been churned from the Milk Ocean.

"Bring her back," called out the seven wise men running from their houses. "Bring her back!"

But Taraka and his demons only screamed in derision and went laughing on their way like a dark comet, pulling the cow with them and leaving chaos and confusion behind.

Taraka had made a mistake in allowing his demons to steal the Sacred Cow. The seven wise men were the children of the mind of Brahma and were close to that

Taraka

Lord of Creation. They came together.

"Shiva must have a son," said Narada.

"But first he must have a wife," said Kasyapa.

"Speak not to me of Shiva," said Daksha with his goat's head. But his six brothers paid him no attention and looking deep inside themselves gave thought to how to find a wife for Shiva.

Now Himavan was the mountain to which Brahma had pulled Manu in his broad boat, and on Himavan lived Himavat, the King of the Himalayas, and his wife Meena. Himavat and Meena had a daughter, Ganga, who, with her deep brown eyes and gurgling laugh, had been born a goddess. Soon they had another daughter, whom they called Uma. Uma was placed in the care of Ganga, so as to keep the growing child close to her and guard her from any harm. From the time that she was born Uma shone and gave out a loving warmth, as if some special fire burned within her. When Ganga looked deep into the child's eyes she saw flames that flickered like tongues of light.

"Those are the flames that consumed the life of Sati," said Ganga to herself, and standing on the peak of Himavan she cried out to the heavens.

"The life of Sati burns in the girl called Uma!"

The gods heard this and pondered on the meaning of it. Taraka heard it in the depths of the ocean and pondered also. The seven wise men looked up to Brahma and he smiled down to them.

Uma

With the life of Sati burning within her, it was no surprise that the first word that Uma uttered was the name of the Lord Shiva.

"Shiva," she called out as she pattered on baby feet through the halls of Himavat's palace.

"Shiva," she called out as she passed through childhood. And still it was the name of Shiva she called when she had become a lovely maiden.

"Go now, Ganga, go on your way," said Uma to her goddess sister one day. "Leave me to find my beloved Shiva." So Ganga left Uma and Uma put her mind to finding Shiva. She sought the help of her father, Himavat.

"You will find Shiva on Kailas," Himavat told her, "but the Lord of Creation sleeps in grief and when you have found him you must ask another to help you wake him. For how to wake him from his frozen slumber, I know not."

"And whom must I ask to help me?" asked Uma.

"I know not that either," said Himavat.

So Uma put on her finest clothes and golden sandals on her feet, and came down from the peak of Himavan. She set off through the mountains to find Shiva's home on Kailas.

The gods saw Uma set out on her journey and called up to Brahma.

"How will she wake him, Lord Brahma – how will she wake the Lord Shiva?"

"I will find a way," said Brahma, and he put his mind to dream upon the matter. Long did Brahma dream with the gods growing anxiously impatient as Uma walked through the mountains in her long search for Shiva. At last Brahma stirred and called down to the gods.

"Bring Kama to me." So the gods brought Kama, who was the God of Love and who rode a green parrot, to stand before Brahma.

"What do you wish, Lord?" asked Kama.

"I wish you to take your bow made of sugar cane with its string made of honeybees and fire an arrow tipped with a flower full of sweetness into the heart of Shiva," said Brahma.

"To what end, Lord?" asked Kama.

"To free him from his frozen sleep," replied Brahma.

"That will need more than my arrow," said Kama. "My arrow will wake him but it will not melt him. If I am to free him I need my wife Rati and my friend Vasanta with me." So Brahma called Rati, the Goddess of Desire, and Vasanta, the God of Springtime, out of the crowd of gods.

"Go now with Kama to the mountain Kailas and when the maiden Uma approaches, awaken Shiva so that he sees her."

Uma

"And how will Uma find Kailas?" they asked.

"You will guide her," replied Brahma. He turned to the rest of the gods and said, "Go now, and leave me."

And so the three left for Kailas and as they left they saw that time, which had stopped when Shiva had settled in his grief, was moving again. Where Vasanta stepped leaves sprung from the trees and where Kama stepped birds sang and where Rati stepped flowers opened and the male and female parts of all things stirred and sought each other.

Meantime Uma had found the track leading upwards to the peak of Kailas. As she walked up the mountainside ever higher and higher the air grew softer, the sun grew warmer, birds sang from the tops of the bushes and everywhere butterflies flitted, soared and glided on shimmering wings.

"Why, spring is here," Uma said to herself, not knowing that Kama and his two companions had been sent by Brahma to await her arrival. Uma picked posies of flowers and set them in her hair. She shook the dust of her travels from her clothes and burnished the gold on her sandals.

"I will come fresh as springtime to my Lord Shiva," she said to herself. "Perhaps I will need no help in waking him."

On she climbed, out of the meadows and up through the forests into the stony wastelands, which led to fields of snow and ice. And, still unseen by Uma, the three kept pace with her and still springtime came with them. Between the boulders and small tufts of grass the mountain plants blazed in blues and golds, the air was alive with the hum of bees, and high above the eagles soared and wheeled and called to each other. At last Uma came to a small hollow amongst the rocks near to the top of the glacier, and there, on the edge of it, sat Shiva, silent as a stone.

"Shiva, my Lord Shiva," whispered Uma, who longed to wake him and yet was afraid to do so.

"Shiva, how I have dreamed of finding you."

But Shiva sat still and unmoving, quite unaware of Uma and the life that stirred all around him.

"How will I wake him?" called Uma to the mountain peaks. But no answer came to her.

"How will I wake him?" she called down to the forests below. But the sound of the wind from the great fir trees carried no message.

"Oh, how will I wake him?" asked Uma to herself in sadness and resignation.

"Now," a voice whispered. It was Vasanta, the God of Springtime, urging Kama to let fly his arrow.

"Now, Kama," added Rati, the Goddess of Desire.

"Now indeed," said Kama and, bending his bow to the full, stroked the wings of the honeybees that made up the bowstring, and shot his flower-tipped arrow straight at the heart of Shiva. Uma heard nothing but a faint hiss and looking up saw Kama's arrow streak through the air and strike the Lord Shiva, embedding its tip deep in his heart.

For a moment nothing happened. Then the Lord Shiva rose slowly to his feet, grasped the arrow by its shaft and, pulling it from his heart, called out.

Uma

"Who wakes me? Who wakes me from my grief?"

Uma gazed up at him in fear and silence. Shiva was angry and this she had not expected.

"Who wakes me?" called Shiva again and again there was no answer.

"If nothing woke me, then nothing shall it be," said Shiva and, ignoring Uma, he turned towards the rocks that hid Kama, Rati and Vasanta, opened up the third eye in his frowning forehead and let fly a blinding, searching flash of light and heat.

Uma was thrown, stunned, to the ground. The flowers fell from her hair, her clothes were scorched by the flames, and all the gold on her lovely sandals turned dull. When she picked herself up and gazed around her she found nothing but desolation. The ground was burnt and charred. The boulders were split. Instead of grass and flowers, small sad wisps of smoke rose from the ground. A cold mist crept down from the mountaintops and wrapped her and all about her in a clammy cloak. There was no sign of Shiva. As she stood in silent disbelief at all that surrounded her, Uma heard a wail of distress.

"Oh, Kama, my beloved husband, and Vasanta my beloved friend, what has become of you?" cried a voice filled with sorrow. Uma looked behind the rocks and found Rati, with torn clothes and tears streaking her face, kneeling beside two small piles of ash.

"Here lie my husband Kama and his lovely parrot, and my friend Vasanta," sobbed Rati, looking up at Uma.

"We were sent by the Lord Brahma to help you waken Shiva," she continued, "and look what happened. Oh what will become of us now?" Rati sobbed and sobbed.

While Rati sobbed, and Uma tried to comfort and console her, they walked slowly and sadly back down the mountain, through the forests, and into the meadows beyond. Now where Rati stepped the flowers stayed closed and nothing stirred with joy.

Taraka the demon had watched all this with great glee.

"A son for Shiva, why Shiva himself has vanished now!" he roared laughing. He rolled about on the ocean floor until the seas slopped over the edge of the earth and salty floods added to the miseries of a world already deprived of love and springtime. Indra and all the other gods were in despair.

"Oh Brahma, Lord Brahma," they called out, "now Shiva is gone and no one knows to where. How will Uma find him now?"

"She will find him by her own path," was all that Brahma would say. Despite all their pleadings he would say no more. The gods, with two of their number now reduced to ashes, watched after Uma as she set off once again through the mountains, leaving Rati to weep her lonely way back to the heavens.

Uma was determined to find Shiva again. She had found him once. She had seen him wake in anger and had seen the full force of his destructive powers blast away Kama and Vasanta and all the signs of springtime, but still she wanted to be with him.

"If he will not stay for me when I come dressed as a bride in spring, then I will follow him dressed as one who will search for a thousand years." And so saying she wrapped herself in a simple homespun cloth all dyed in yellow ochre, and put rush sandals on her feet. As she walked on and on, up the mountains, down the rocky valleys, across burning deserts and icy streams and through the years, she said quietly all the time, "Shiva, I come to you."

Uma

The gods heard these words and, remembering how Ganga had called out that the life of Sati was burning in Uma, they hoped. At last, one day, Uma came into a forest glade, and there found an old man sitting on a rock. He was a wandering yogi, orange-robed and all creased with age.

"Blessings, daughter," called out the old man.

"Blessings, father," replied Uma. "Can you put me on the road to the Lord Shiva?"

"Shiva, what would you want with him?" asked the yogi in great surprise.

"I have sought him all my life," said Uma, "and I will go on to seek him until I find him, even if it takes forever."

"But child," said the yogi, "Shiva has vanished and even if you find him you will not turn him from his love of death and all that goes with it. Forget Shiva, he is not worth finding."

"You are wrong, father," replied Uma, "there is great beauty in the Lord Shiva. Without the works of Shiva, the Lord Brahma would stop creating lest the world become too full. Although the nature of Shiva is destruction, he is also a Lord of Creation."

"So say you!" called a great voice. Uma looked up into a blaze of light, and saw standing in the place of the old yogi the great Lord Shiva.

"By those words, by your simple clothes, and by your ceaseless searching I know that the life of my beloved Sati burns in you," said Shiva. Taking Uma's hand in his he set his face towards the distant peaks and Kailas.

Uma's search was over. The gods, seeing this, laughed loudly in their pleasure.

Their laughter woke Rati from her slumber of despair and, hearing the cause of it, she went to find Shiva and Uma.

"Please Lord, please forgive my husband and return him to me, and also my friend the springtime."

"Why should I?" asked Shiva remembering with anger how he had been woken by Kama's dart.

"Because they came to help me wake you," Uma interjected, "and without their help you might be silent on Kailas still."

So Shiva, knowing that Kama and Vasanta had meant no harm and that it was he himself who had made Uma prove her love for him, restored Kama and Vasanta to life again. And as the spirits of love and springtime were rejoined with Rati they skipped and sang together through the world, so that all became joyful again and everywhere was filled with the sound of song and dance, and the smell of sandalwood, and everything was splashed with young fresh colour.

Shiva and Uma gave a great feast at their marriage and all the gods came, bringing gifts and blessings.

"A thunderbolt to guard your gates," said Indra.

"A breeze to cool you," said Vayu, the Wind God.

"A flame to warm you," said Agni, the Fire God.

"The coolest water to quench your thirst," said Ganga.

"A thousand pearls to feed your souls," said Kubera, the God of Wealth.

Uma

"Shells for your floor," said Varuna, the God of the Oceans.

"A blanket to cover you," said Ratri, the Goddess of Night.

"Roses to put in your cheeks," said Ushas to Uma, and so it went on until the peak of Kailas swayed and bent, so great was the weight of gifts upon it.

"Soon," said Indra, "soon shall Shiva and Uma have a son and then will we be freed of that tyrant Taraka!" With that happy thought the gods streamed home from Kailas sure that before long their fear of Taraka would be in the past.

Kartikeya

Kartikeya

Shiva and Uma had been married many years, but still they had no child. The gods were puzzled but Taraka the demon was not.

"Shiva can hold the lovely Uma to him until the end of time but no child will come of it," chuckled Taraka. "Even though Shiva is a Lord of Creation, it is destruction which is in his nature. Nothing can he begin and nothing will he beget."

Taraka was right and he knew it. Although he had lain and watched events in quietness as Uma sought Shiva, now he gathered his demon hordes and again raided and burned the kingdoms of the gods.

Trampled and bruised, the gods went to Brahma.

"Taraka burns our houses, and the house of Shiva is filled with the gifts we gave him and nothing more," said Indra.

"With what should the house of Shiva be filled?" asked Brahma.

"With children!" said Agni the Fire God, who was a great maker of children.

"Then tell him so," said Brahma.

Tales of Destruction

"Yes, tell Shiva," said the seven wise men, who had also come to Brahma. So Agni joined hands with his brother the sun and sailed across the heavens to find Shiva on the peak of Kailas. As they neared the mountain they passed over a glade deep in the forest where Shiva had lately been with his beloved Uma.

Agni's piercing gaze lit up the leafy clearing and in it shone a speck, a twinkling point of light that beckoned to the god.

"A seed of Shiva!" exclaimed Agni, and turning himself into a pure white dove he came down from the sky and took the seed of Shiva in his beak. With clapping wings he raced through the skies back to the palace of Indra.

"Now, with a seed of Shiva can we surely make him a son," thought Agni. But as the bird flew, the seed, though it was no larger than the smallest pearl, grew heavier and heavier. Slower and slower Agni flew with failing strength until at last, unable to bear the weight, he opened his beak and let the seed of Shiva fall. Down and down it fell, gleaming like the finest gem until, just as the dove was transformed back into the Fire God, it settled on a sandy shore of the River Ganges.

"What did Shiva say?" asked Indra.

"He said we must wait in patience," replied Agni, ashamed to admit what had happened and hoping that he might yet find the seed again. But hard as he searched through the shores of the Ganges, he could see no sign of it.

The reason that Agni could not find the seed of Shiva was this: no sooner had it fallen from the skies than the goddess Ganga had secretly gathered it up and hidden it deep in the flowing waters of her river.

Tales of Destruction

There Ganga looked hard and long at the seed of Shiva, and when she saw that it would grow into a male child she called down six of the fullest breasted stars to give it secret suckle. Fast the baby grew on that starry milk, and as he grew so Ganga taught him the wisdom of the ages and sang him the songs of the gods and of creation. And as he grew so the seed of light grew within him, until his brilliance burst from the confines of his river home and told the world and the gods of his presence.

"Who is he, this Lord of Light?" asked his six foster mothers of the goddess Ganga.

"He is beautiful as the moon and bright as the sun, and his name is Kartikeya," replied Ganga.

"And who is his father?" asked Indra, looking down from his palace walls.

"He is the child of Shiva," called back Ganga.

"Now we will be revenged!" cheered the gods. And Agni, who had known the answer to Indra's question all along, still kept his secret to himself. He went to Saraswati, the wife of Brahma, to ask for the gift of a peacock for Kartikeya to ride upon.

Great was the rejoicing in the heavens when Kartikeya, with flowing golden hair and clad in brilliant silver armour, rode into the courtyard of Indra's palace on the back of the peacock given to him by Saraswati. Proudly the peacock spread his tail and from each feathered eye there sprang a fearsome warrior, fully armed. More and more did Kartikeya's army grow until the heavens rang and rang again with the clang of metal striking metal and with the excited roars of the gods.

Suddenly a cry went up. "Taraka, Taraka is coming!"

Chandra, the Moon God, peered over the edge of heaven as the day approached its end.

Kartikeya

He had seen the demon horde come streaming like a smoking cloud from the caves of the nether regions. Led by Taraka, the demons sought the source of all this noise and clamour, and now they prepared to fight.

Great was the battle between the gods and demons. Bravely the demons fought but Kartikeya and his peacock warriors cut and hewed and scythed through throngs of bat-faced monsters, until finally Kartikeya came face to face with Taraka.

"Who am I?" cried Kartikeya as he knocked the demon to the ground.

"Who am I?" cried Kartikeya again, as he pressed the point of his sword against the demon's throat.

"Who are you?" gasped Taraka.

"I am the son of Shiva," answered Kartikeya, with an awful smile. As he said this he reached down and picked the demon up from the ground by one ear and, holding him wriggling at arm's length, sliced his head from his shoulders. He let it fall, bouncing and rolling down from the battlefield on the edge of heaven, down through the world and back into the nether regions from whence Taraka had come.

"Now is my promise kept," said Brahma. And Kartikeya stayed in the kingdom of the gods and became the God of War.

How Uma Became Parvati

Now Uma knew that Kartikeya was Shiva's child and she was not pleased.

"Why do you not give me a child?" she asked of Shiva. "Why is this new god Kartikeya born from your seed grown in the river of my sister Ganga? Why does your seed not grow in me?"

"Because it does not and it will not," answered Shiva.

"How did you give your seed to my sister Ganga?" asked Uma.

"I know not," said Shiva. And this was true because he did not know how Agni had found the seed lying on the forest floor. Uma persisted with her questioning until the Lord Shiva stamped his foot so that the sides of Kailas shook.

"Enough," he said.

"Enough?" cried Uma. "It is not enough, it is not enough of anything. If it is enough then let it be enough for the wives of Brahma and Vishnu. Let Saraswati and Lakshmi be barren also."

"That is a fearful curse," Shiva warned.

"Then give me a child and make me undo it," said Uma.

"I have said that my seed cannot and will not grow in you," said Shiva, and he stamped his foot again so that in the heavens and in the world and in the underworld all knew that he and Uma quarrelled.

"Undo the curse on Saraswati and Lakshmi," demanded Shiva.

"I will," said Uma, "but first you will see me dance the dance of my darkest nature. It is not only you, Lord, who is a destroyer."

And Uma loosened her hair so that it fell about her shoulders, slipped her sandals from her feet and began. Slowly at first and then faster she spun and swayed until she became lost and mad in the joy and rhythm of her dance. Round and round she spun on flying feet and Shiva watching saw her take first the form of Durga the beautiful warrior goddess with her fists full of fearsome weapons given to her by the gods. Then the flying blur that Uma had become took on a darker hue and became the hideous goddess Kalee, the Destroyer of Time, her mouth full of wild cries, a third eye in the centre of her head, her fingers dripping blood and her naked body wrapped in her long black hair. Then, as Uma's dance slowed again the blackness of Kalee's skin paled and faded and she became the softly curving Jagadgauri, the Goddess of Harvests.

"This last I have shown you to remind you that fruitfulness is also in me," said Uma, and as she had promised, her dance done, she lifted the curse from Saraswati and Lakshmi.

From that time, Shiva looked upon Uma with great uneasiness. The flash of temper and the curse followed by her wild, unbridled dance had shown Shiva a different side of Uma. It seemed to him that her clear skin was now and then tinged with the dark tones of Kalee, that lover of blood and sacrifice. Close as destruction was to Shiva's

own nature, he preferred the pure devoted love of Uma, and of Sati whose life burned in Uma.

One day, Shiva was reading aloud to Uma from one of the books of creation when he saw that she was sleeping.

"Is that not so?" he asked Uma in a loud voice.

"Why yes, Lord," said Uma, startled into guilty wakefulness.

"Is that not what?" persisted Shiva, pressing his advantage.

"I know not," admitted Uma, blushing with shame.

"Since you are so fond of curses, now will I put one on you," said Shiva. "So you will learn to catch my words, go and spend some time making nets like the fishermen." And with those words Shiva put his hand under the edge of the stool on which Uma sat and tipped it, and Uma with it, over the edge of Kailas.

Down and down spun Uma, growing smaller and younger as she slid through the skies until, as no more than a year-old babe, she fell to earth on the shores of the eastern ocean. There her bawling attracted the attention of a fisherman and his wife who took the child into their home.

"We will call her Parvati," said the fisherman, and his wife agreed.

As the years passed and Parvati grew beautiful and golden-skinned as the sands she had fallen upon, so Shiva tried to forget her. He knew that Parvati making and mending nets on the shore was Uma living out the curse he had placed upon her, but he tried to put her out from his mind.

"Uma has gone and Parvati I will not have," he said to himself as he settled again

How Uma Became Parvati

on the peak of Kailas and tried to regain the frozen peace that Kama had interrupted many springtimes before.

It was no use. Try as he might his mind turned to the beauty of Parvati on the seashore below. Shiva itched and burned at the very thought of her. Finally, he decided to make Parvati his and he sent a great shark to break and tear the nets of the fisher folk with whom Parvati lived.

The weeks and months went by and the fisher folk became poorer as their catches vanished, and when they should have been fishing they gave their time instead to mending the gaping holes in their nets. All the young fishermen were in love with Parvati, and finally the chief of the fishermen declared that she would be given in marriage to the fisherman who would end the tyranny of the marauding shark.

This was the opportunity that Shiva had sought to create. Taking the form of a bold and handsome young fisherman, he came down to earth, leapt from the seashore into the boiling surf, sent the shark thrumming and scudding in fright back to the depths of the oceans and, claiming Parvati as his bride, returned with her to Kailas.

There on Kailas, Parvati, in whom burned the lives of Sati and Uma, settled to become the wife of Shiva through all the ages that were to come. Shiva took care not to anger Parvati. He remembered Uma becoming Durga and Kalee and her wild black dance and as he gazed at Parvati's beautiful golden skin he thought to himself, "Now Uma has become Parvati, let her stay as Parvati."

Ganesha

Parvati's beauty was of a rare and unusual kind. It lay not in the softness
of her features, the gloss on her hair, the golden glow of her skin, nor in
the way she walked. It came instead from deep within. She had a glow
of joyfulness that shone through her eyes and skin and warmed everyone
who saw her. When Parvati came out of her apartment in the mornings and walked
to join Shiva in the halls of that palace of ice, the radiance which shone from her leapt
from the walls to the pillars and out of the palace and back again.

"She is beautiful," said Shiva. And to himself quietly he would add, "How I wish
I knew where her beauty came from."

Parvati treasured her beauty and the cause of it. That cause was her secret and it lay
in her bathing room. As she sat in her bath early in the morning while the sky was
turning from blue through green to rose and gold and the parakeets had not yet begun
to fly, she turned her eyes deep into the corners of her mind and sought out the nature
of her being. Parvati loved that time, and the peace that search gave her stayed deep
within her, burning joyfully through every part of her and lasting through the day.

Parvati knew that Shiva wanted to know the secret of her beauty. And although he was her husband and she loved him greatly, she knew her beauty was her own and that she must keep its secret safe.

"What do you do in your bathing room?" asked Shiva one day.

"Why, I bathe, holy one," answered Parvati.

"But you do more than that," said Shiva. The words were part statement, part question, and they troubled Parvati. She knew that before long Shiva would come to her bathing room door and ask for entry.

"If only I had a son to hold the door," she said to herself as she sat in her bath the next morning. As the words went through her mind so her hand strayed to her left foot where it lay next to her lap. With her fingers she kneaded the sole of her foot and as she squeezed and rubbed, little rolls of water-soft skin came loose and lay in her palm like slim pencils. Idly she picked them out and rolled them first into a ball, then into a shape and finally into a minute human form.

"You have your son," she said to herself, and stepping from her bath, she sprinkled the tiny grey form that lay in her hand with water from the River Ganges that she kept in a glass bottle amongst the perfumes and oils in her toilet box. So sprinkled, the babe grew and in no time stood bearded and moustached, a fine warrior with his hand held firm upon the bathing room door.

Before many days had passed, Shiva left his bed in the early dawn and went to visit Parvati as she bathed. Finding the door tight shut he pushed and pushed until he had made a small gap. Putting his eye close up against the edge of the door, he saw not the soft round form of Parvati but the curling beard and hard limbs of her son.

"Who is this?" he shouted in a great rage.

"He is my son, holy one," answered Parvati.

"You may have no child without my blessing!" said Shiva.

"He is the son of my body and my mind," said Parvati. "He is mine alone and I need no blessing."

Furious, Shiva forced the door, took a sword from his belt and with a mighty bow struck the young man's head off so that it rolled away to a far corner of the bathing room. But the headless body remained standing and from out of its neck burst a fountain of pure water.

"Water!" exclaimed Shiva. "No blood?"

"It is the purest blood of all," said Parvati. "It is the blood that flows from the spirits of the gods. It is the water of the River Ganges."

"How can I stem it?" asked Shiva who was by now panicking, ashamed of his bad temper and the result of it.

"You must do three things," said Parvati.

"What are they?" asked Shiva.

"First," said Parvati, "you must ask my forgiveness."

"I do so," said Shiva.

"I will forgive you if you do the other two things," Parvati continued.

"And if I do not?" asked Shiva.

"Then," said Parvati, "the waters of the Ganges will flow through this place until there is nothing at all but rocks and sand and not the smallest trace of your palace."

"I will do the two things," said Shiva.

"You must promise never again to come to my bathing room," said Parvati.

"I promise," said Shiva. "And the other thing?"

"You must take the head from the first living creature you see and give it to my son in place of the one you struck from him."

"And then I will have your forgiveness?" asked Shiva.

"Most surely," replied Parvati.

The Lord Shiva strode from the bathing room, out through the palace halls and into the courtyard. There stood the kitchen elephant waiting patiently, while the sacks of roots he had brought in from the fields were unloaded into the palace cellars.

"A great future for you, my friend – and a surprise for Parvati!" chuckled Shiva as, for the second time that morning, he took his sword and cut a head from its body. Taking the elephant's head by its trunk, Shiva went back to the bathing room where, before Parvati could say a word, the body of her son and the head of the elephant united so that not a join could be seen.

"So be it," said Parvati, quietly.

"So be it," said Shiva. He was pleased with himself and for the moment had forgotten why he had come to Parvati's bathing room at all.

The kitchen rat had followed the head of his friend the elephant on its journey through the palace.

"That body is too small for so large a head," he said, and offered himself as an extra set of legs.

Parvati continued in beauty and knew herself more and more. Shiva was irked by the knowledge that the secret of Parvati's beauty lay in her bathing room and must remain there, but he kept his promise and stayed away from Parvati in the early morning.

And Parvati's elephant-headed son rode out of the palace on the back of the kitchen rat. Parvati had forgotten to give her son a name, but the world called him Ganesha and he, in his turn, became a great god.

Yama and the Love Girl

Of all the gods, the one to whom Shiva felt closest was Yama, God of Death. Yama would go wherever in the world that Shiva bade him. And so it was that on a fine day in early spring Yama heard the call of Shiva, and left his home in the South. With him he brought his big black water buffalo and his two fierce black hounds, each with four eyes. As he walked he plaited a length of rope. The rope was made from the longest hairs in the water buffalo's tail, and each time Yama plucked a handful from the tuft, more hairs grew in their place.

Slowly, Yama crossed the countryside with his long strides. The sun was full on him but he and his beasts cast no shadow, for they had none. He was in no hurry and now and then he paused and looked round at the world with his deep green eyes.

"How beautiful all creatures are," he said to himself. "How nice it is that their spirits all come to me so that I can look after them." He smiled a long secret smile at a tiger club nuzzling milk from the belly of its black and gold mother.

"Even you, little stripes, even you," he murmured.

In the evening of that day, Yama came to a clearing in the forest. Sitting by the trunk of a fallen tree was a beautiful girl cradling the head of a young man, who lay still in her lap.

"I have come for the spirit of your husband," said Yama. "You are a good and loving wife, but you must give him up to me now." And he made a running noose in the rope he had plaited.

"Wait, Lord," said the girl, "wait just a minute, please. We have been married only a year. A moment, while I look a little longer at him."

"I cannot wait," said Yama. "It is over and now I must go." As he spoke he plucked the young man's spirit loose, slipped the noose around its neck and turned, ready to pull the feather-light burden back to the Land of the Dead.

"Wait, Lord," pleaded the girl again.

"What now?" asked Yama.

"Lord, since my spirit is still with me, how is it that I can see you?" asked the girl. "And hear you also?"

"You have great insight," said Yama. "Only humans with a fine and clear view into the heart of things can see the gods." And he began to walk on with his water buffalo and black hounds padding softly behind him. But the girl followed after them.

On and on they walked, deeper into the South, deeper into the night, through forests, over hills, across rivers, and always south. Finally they were on a cold grey path, with Yama still leading and the rope tensed over his shoulder. The rest followed behind with the young man's spirit bumping between, and the girl last of all. Yama turned and faced the girl.

Yama and the Love Girl

"You must leave us here. You have followed your husband's spirit in its journey as a good wife, but at the next turn in the track is the beginning of my kingdom." He jerked his head to show where everything disappeared into mist and puffs of wind up ahead.

"I hear you, Lord," said the girl. But still she followed after Yama, through the mist and wind, into Yama's kingdom. There the water buffalo stopped still and the hounds growled. Yama turned.

"What are you thinking of, girl?" he asked. "This is the Land of the Dead, you may not follow here."

"I have no fear of death, Lord," said the girl. "It simply follows life and it is my wish to be with my husband."

"But," said Yama, "you are not allowed here. You are live; your spirit is still within you. The living are not allowed in the Land of the Dead."

"Maybe not," said the girl, "but if my love bids me to stay with my husband and yet it is true that I may not stay in this deathly place, then the solution is in your hands, Lord."

"And how?" asked Yama.

"By returning my husband to me," replied the girl.

"Oh no," said Yama. "A spirit may not return. It is not allowed. Once a spirit has come to me it can only go onwards to another life."

"Then we both have a problem," she said.

"People may not argue with me. That is not allowed either," said Yama. "Be off with you." And he turned and went on his way pulling the young man's spirit deeper and deeper into his kingdom.

"What a strange girl," he said to himself. "So unafraid of death." This thought warmed Yama. There was great kindness in him and it saddened him when his arrival caused pain or fear.

"I will miss her, a little." As this thought wandered through his mind he heard a light footstep behind him. The water buffalo snorted and the four-eyed hounds growled once more. Yama turned and, again, there the girl stood with one hand resting on a boulder beside the path.

"What do you want, foolish girl? It is not possible for you to be here. This is the Land of the Dead!"

"You know very well why I am here, Lord," said the girl.

Yama felt a little flick of anger, and of anxiety. She was a nice and unusual girl and he liked her courage. But the other gods would be watching and if they saw him unable to rule his own kingdom, they would laugh at him for a million years.

"Go home, girl," he said, as firmly as he could.

"No, Lord," said the girl.

"Go home before I set my hounds on you." Yama narrowed his eyes to make them as cold and cruel as possible.

"I know you will not set them on me," said the girl. "I do not fear them any more than I fear you."

"Everyone is afraid of me," said Yama.

"But they need not be," she replied.

Yama thought for a minute. If fear would not persuade the girl to go, perhaps a gift would.

"I admire greatly your courage and devotion," he said, making himself as tall and important as possible, "and to ease your path out of my kingdom, I will make you a gift. You may have anything you wish, except the spirit of your husband."

"I wish nothing for myself but my husband," said the girl. "But if I may not have him, then I would like something that would be pleasing to him. My husband's father is blind – please, Lord, give the old man back his sight."

"Granted child," said Yama. "Your selflessness does you credit – now go in peace and please that old man's eyes with your beauty." And Yama turned from her and began to walk on.

"That was the right way to deal with her," he thought. But his pleasure at solving the problem was tinged a little with regret. It was not often he met people so unafraid of him.

"Perhaps she can see the kindness in me," he thought. "Or perhaps her love for her husband stems her fear – perhaps it's both. Perhaps she has even a little love for me as well as for her husband." With that very human thought, Yama, the God of Death, set his head into the gloom and resolved to put the girl from his mind.

"She is a witch," he thought. "She not only invades my kingdom, but she has got into my mind as well."

The path seemed steeper than usual, and the shadows darker. Although he knew

Yama and the Love Girl

he should feel nothing but a stern anger, Yama felt a small glow of pleasure when he turned a corner in the path to find the girl sitting in a pool of light amidst the darkness.

Summoning all his willpower, Yama cried, "I sent you home! What are you doing wandering about in my kingdom? It's unheard of! Besides, it is ungrateful of you to have stayed after my gift."

"I didn't say I would go, Lord," said the girl quietly.

"Well," said Yama, "if I offer you another gift will you go then?"

"I'll think about it," came the reply.

"Think about it carefully," said Yama sternly. "Now tell me what you wish. I will give it to you provided it is not the spirit of your husband."

"My husband's parents are very poor," said the girl. "It would have pleased my husband to know they had enough money to make their old age easier."

"Granted," said Yama quickly. He did not pause to praise the girl this time.

"Now go. The path ahead is very steep and you were wise to choose this place to leave us." And Yama pulled the spirit of the young man to the side of the water buffalo and draped it across the beast's back.

"Keep close to me now," he commanded his dogs, and up and away he went. Higher and higher Yama climbed, up to the bottom of the wet grey clouds and beyond. But before long Yama realised the girl was still following him.

"Wait," he commanded the water buffalo. "You have deceived me, girl. You promised to leave."

"I said I would think about it."

"But you said it with a half promise in your voice…"

"That, Lord, was in your mind, not in my voice," came the soft reply.

"This time," said Yama, "I have nothing but hardship to give you – you have followed me when I told you you may not." And, turning away from the girl, he urged the water buffalo into a fast pace.

"Now she must suffer," he said to himself. "Love is all very well, but this refusal to obey the laws of life and death has gone too far." So Yama chose the hardest road to the South. Up the steepest slopes, through the hottest deserts, across the foulest marshes, under the surface of the deepest lakes and even into the caves of ice at the tops of the mountains went Yama. And still the girl followed. Her feet blistered, her clothes tore and her hair hung in sweat-stained tangles down her back, but still she followed.

Eventually Yama stopped. He was feeling the strain of the journey himself and he wished to take the quickest and quietest route to the heart of his kingdom. He could not shake the girl off and deep inside he knew that the harder he made the way for her, the more determined she was to follow.

"I'll try to weaken her with gifts one more time," he decided.

"Child," he said, turning to her. "You know you may not have the spirit of your husband, but if you promise to leave for ever I will grant you a third and last wish."

"My husband would have liked sons, Lord," said the girl. "Tell me that I will be the bearer of one hundred sons for my husband and I will go."

"They are yours," said Yama. "Are you sure one hundred will be enough?"

Yama and the Love Girl

"Lord," said the girl, "you have stretched my love until it nearly broke but now I believe I have won."

"Won? What do you mean?" asked Yama.

"Lord, how may I bear even one son for my husband without him to help me in the making of children?"

Yama felt a great surge of anger rise in him, but even as it reached his throat it was followed by honest laughter. Outwitted, and by an obstinate wand of a girl!

"Child," he said smiling. "You have won indeed and you have won by the love you have for your husband. Take him back to life and make yourselves a hundred sons." And so Yama untied the noose at the end of his plaited rope and placed the spirit in the girl's outstretched arms.

"After all," mused Yama, as he watched the small figure fade into the North, "they will both come back to me and their one hundred sons after them."

Hanuman

Hanuman

One of the most beautiful of the maidens who had danced in the sky on the way to Indra's palace was named Anjana. And Anjana was as naughty as she was beautiful. She put straws up the trunks of Indra's elephants to make them sneeze. She pulled feathers from the tail of Saraswati's peacock. She galloped wildly through the skies on the back of the milk white stallion. She even stole a sip from the golden goblet that the gods kept their ambrosia in.

"Anjana, you will come to a bad end," warned Ganesha, waving his trunk at her.

"One day you will be caught," warned the rat that Ganesha was riding on. And finally, one day, she was caught. On a dark night when clouds were scudding across the face of the sky, she snuck into the fields of the seven wise men and lay under the sacred cow to steal her milk. There she fell asleep. And when the seven wise men came in the morning to milk the cow they found her udders dry, and the beautiful thief curled up in a tussock of grass close beside the beast. Roundly the seven wise men cursed Anjana.

"Anjana," they declared, "Anjana, we all have had enough of your pranks. We all have had enough of your teasing and your stealing. Now you will find that the reward for mischief is a long tail!" They threw her from the sky, and down, down, down she fell into the tops of the mountains, until she landed with a great bump on a peak named Himalchuli, which means the cliff of ice.

When Anjana picked herself up she found that she had become furry all over and had a long, long tail. The seven wise men had turned her into a monkey.

Shortly after Anjana fell from the sky onto the peak of Himalchuli, a king in a distant country was seeking to make children with his three wives. On the advice of a yogi he had summoned to help him, he had made three sweet cakes out of sugar, rice and melted butter.

"Give your wives these cakes, oh King, and in return they will give you children," said the yogi.

So at dawn the next day the king called his three wives to him and gave to each of them one of the cakes he had made. And for each of them, as directed by the yogi, he made a spell.

"May this cake make you fruitful, beloved wife."

The youngest of the king's wives was the third and last to receive a cake. Distracted by her displeasure at being the third in line, she barely noticed when a hawk swooped down, snatched the cake from her hands and flew away with it.

On and on the hawk flew, out of the country of the king, over forests, over lakes and rivers, over the wide burning plains, and up towards the high snow-covered mountains. Soon the hawk approached the peak of Himalchuli, on which Anjana sat,

wondering at the length of her tail and remembering what the seven wise men had said to her.

"A long tail is a poor reward," she said to herself. She looked longingly up at her sisters dancing in the sky in their thousands, and wondered how long she would have to stay as a monkey alone on that mountain top.

As she looked at her sisters in the sky, the hawk carrying the sweet cake with the yogi's spell flew overhead. Anjana was very hungry, and leapt from the mountain peak with outstretched paws to grab the cake and take it from the bird. The hawk, startled from his steady flight, jinked to one side and let go of the cake. He flew quickly on his way, leaving Anjana chattering with rage and disappointment and watching the cake as it fell and fell into the valley below.

It happened that Vayu, the Wind God, was passing by. Greatly struck by the beauty of the girl monkey on the snowy peak, he swooped down into the valley and catching up the cake brought it to Anjana. As she opened her mouth to eat the cake, Vayu blew into her throat and down into her being and made a child with her.

No sooner had Vayu left her than Anjana began to swell with the child in her. All through the day she swelled and swelled and in the evening the child was born. Vayu looked down from far away and watched Anjana suckle her fine furry monkey child.

"His name is Hanuman," Vayu called out to the heavens. "His name is Hanuman and he will fly with the gods and he will talk with the gods. He will have the swiftness of the wind and when he lashes his tail the oceans will boil and the forests will be flattened so that even Rudra, the God of Storms, will hide from him."

All through the night Anjana fed Hanuman and all through the night Hanuman grew until, as morning approached, he had grown so much that the top of Himalchuli was flattened with the weight of him. He was now too large for Anjana to feed and instead of sitting in her lap he held her cupped in one paw.

When the sun rose above the mists that filled the mountain valleys and hung in the sky as a great golden ball, the giant Hanuman mistook it for an orange, and stretched out his paw to take it. Terrified, the sun spun up into the heavens, with Hanuman bouncing after him. The chase went up through the highest peaks and into the kingdoms of the excited gods, until at last Indra came out of his palace to see what all the noise was about.

"Who wakes me on this afternoon?" called Indra and, cheered on by the other gods, took up a thunderbolt from the corner of his palace courtyard and threw it at Hanuman.

Such was the force of the blow that it made a hole in Hanuman's jaw, knocking off the corner of one tooth and sending him reeling through the sky and back down to the earth below. As Hanuman fell he opened the paw in which he was holding Anjana. In a flash, Anjana wriggled free and fled to rejoin her sisters in the sky on the way to Indra's palace. There she hid hoping the seven wise men would not notice her return.

When Vayu, the God of Wind, saw his son Hanuman limping about on earth holding a sore jaw, he was angry. He was angry with Indra and he was angry with all the other gods.

"Now they will feel my anger," he muttered. In his vengeful mood he entered the stomachs of all the gods so that they were filled with gripe and discomfort. Great was the misery of the gods as they tottered around on unsteady legs holding their swollen bellies as Vayu rolled and rumbled inside them.

"You must put an end to this, Indra," gasped Ganesha, who was especially badly afflicted and whose rounded stomach was tight as a drum.

"Yes," added Rudra. "Tempests on the outside are one thing. Tempests on the inside are quite another."

So Indra, in discomfort and shame, called out to Vayu, "What must I do to ease our suffering?"

Vayu answered, "First must you humbly ask Hanuman's pardon."

Indra did so.

Then Vayu said, "Now must you make his jaw whole and grant him eternal life."

And Indra did that also.

Then Vayu said, "That was well done. Now indeed will my son fly and talk with the gods for the rest of time."

And Vayu left the stomachs of all the gods as a great wind and they lived in comfort again.

Hanuman, with his jaw mended, now started on a life of high adventure. Able to make himself large or small at any moment, and with the speed of wind that his father had given him and the strength of a giant, he bounded along as he pleased, doing many great and wonderful things. The entire world came to know of Hanuman and to hear of his adventures.

Chandra's Shame

Chandra's Shame

You will remember how Ganesha, the god with the head of an elephant joined to the body of a man, went out into the world from the palace of Shiva riding on the back of the kitchen rat. Into all manner of places Ganesha went, from the peaks of the mountains in the North to the glowing opal beaches in the South, and always accompanied by his faithful friend the rat. Sometimes on these journeys the rat became tired and Ganesha dismounted and either set himself under a tree to sleep while the rat rested or, if there was no time for sleeping, walked for himself with the rat trailing along behind. When Ganesha walked for himself the other gods always put their mouths behind their hands to conceal their tittering smiles. In truth, Ganesha was a comic sight. His head was the size of his body and half again and, unless he remembered to keep it carefully curled, his trunk would trail on the ground and become entangled in his feet as he tottered along with tiny steps. But the other gods were careful not to laugh out loud. Ganesha had sharp ears and a reputation for laying about him, placing curses on the heads of those who displeased him.

Tales of Destruction

One day, Ganesha was walking for himself through Chandraloka, that being the name of the place in the heavens where Chandra, the God of the Moon, dwells. Ganesha was concentrating so much on not tripping over his trunk that, looking behind him to check his friend was following, he tripped instead on a stone and fell flat on his back in the middle of a large black puddle.

Chandra, who of all the gods had the roughest and strongest sense of fun, happened to be looking on and let out a great guffaw.

"Ho, Elephant Head," he called, "I hope the skin your mother gave you is thick enough to stand that wallop!"

Now this remark about the thickness of Ganesha's skin referred to his very beginning when his mother, Parvati, fashioned him from rolls of skin rubbed from the sole of her foot. Ganesha was especially sensitive to remarks about his beginnings and, rolling himself first on to his stomach and then using his trunk as a crutch, he pushed himself back on to his feet and looked about him.

"Who said that?" he called out, his trunk raised in challenge.

"I did," said Chandra, stepping out from behind the moon, "and before you say any more, you need to use that trunk of yours to clean down your backside; there's a lot of mud on it."

"I think you should apologise," said Ganesha.

"What for?" asked Chandra. "It's you who woke everyone up falling around the place, not me. Sit down on your rat again, the poor little chap."

He was already annoyed, but this remark about his good friend made Ganesha really

very angry. Just like anybody else, he did not like to be reminded that he relied so much on the help of someone smaller and weaker than him. And, as with anybody else, a bruised pride turned easily to anger.

"Chandra," he called out, "Chandra, shame on you for your laughter at my misfortune. Shame on you for mocking my mother, and shame on you for sneering at my friend. I curse you, Chandra! And my curse is this: from this day all who see you will feel guilt, although they have done no wrong."

And so Ganesha, with his trunk curled and his mouth set, sat down on the back of the rat and, without a further glance at the moon god, passed from Chandraloka.

At first, Chandra paid little attention to Ganesha's curse. But then he began to notice that in his presence gods, people and animals looked uncomfortable. Their eyes shifted in their faces and they slipped into the shadows as far away from Chandra as they could get. Soon Chandra was the loneliest god in all the heavens and, unable to bear the shame Ganesha had laid on him, he hid himself deep within the comforting petals of a lotus flower.

The other gods missed Chandra. Chandraloka was usually a merry place and Chandra's laughter cheered all who came there. Further, Ganesha's curse was not only visited on Chandra, it was visited on all who saw him. Guilt is painful enough, but guilt without real cause is a scorching torment that everyone can do without. Indra and the other older gods summoned Ganesha.

"Ganesha," they said, "we are older than you, we were old in the sky when Parvati, your mother, first dreamed of you in her bathing room. Undo the curse you have placed on Chandra and all who see him."

Chandra's Shame

"No," said Ganesha.

"Ganesha," they repeated, "we are older than you, we were old in the sky when Parvati fashioned you in her fingers. Undo the cruse you have placed on Chandra and all who see him."

"No," said Ganesha for the second time.

"Ganesha," they said, "we are older than you, we were old in the sky when Shiva gave you your elephant head. Yet, even though we are older than you, if you will undo the curse, we and all the gods will bow our heads before you."

"Do it," said Ganesha.

So Indra and the other gods bowed their heads before Ganesha.

"Let Chandra bow also," said Ganesha. So Indra sent the youngest of the other gods to fetch Chandra from out of the heart of the lotus flower. And when he came, with pollen from the lotus blossoms on his shoulders, Indra made him bow his head before Ganesha.

"Now will you undo the curse on Chandra?" they asked.

"Yes, and no," said Ganesha.

"And what does that mean?" Indra and the other gods asked. By now they were becoming impatient with the darkness in Ganesha.

"I release Chandra from the curse," said Ganesha, "except in this. I declare this day to be the day of Chandra's shame and every god and every person and every creature and every demon that sees Chandra on this day in every year from now until the end of this world shall feel the pangs of guilt."

"Even though they have done no wrong? And forever? That is a terrible thing. There is no mercy in you, Ganesha!" all the gods and Chandra cried.

"So they shall feel," Ganesha said, with a wave of his trunk that showed finality.

The day on which Ganesha spoke his final word on the matter was the first day of harvest. And from that time all men who are out at night, when the corn is ripe and the sky holds the thin faint strip that is the last of the summer moons, have bowed three times and said,

"Chandra, stay hidden lest we feel your shame."

Tales of Preservation

The Blue Boy

The Blue Boy

As hundreds of years passed after the beginning of this world, and all the creatures and all the plants and everything which was in the world multiplied and increased so that the world was full, there came a time when mankind cried up to the Lords Brahma and Vishnu and Shiva and said, "It is enough."

And Brahma looked down and asked, "Who is this that says it is enough?"

"It is we, Lord Brahma, we who have built a million temples in honour of your name."

And Brahma said, "If you built a hundred million temples in my name, still you may not say 'it is enough'. I am the first Lord of Creation, and the Creator of the world and all that is in it and all that will be in it. For me it can never be enough."

And Shiva came down from Mount Kailas and, standing at the side of Brahma, said;

"I too am a Lord of Creation and I am the Destroyer. For so long as there is creation, so must I destroy. Though you may honour me with worship from now until the end of time, for me it can never be enough."

Tales of Preservation

❧ 🙶

And the mind of Shiva dreamt of the terrible Kalee and she appeared in the world and danced in all her black triumphant horridness on the steps of the temples and on the graves. And men saw the blood dripping from her fingers and were afraid. Then spoke Vishnu;

"Mankind, of creation and destruction there can never be enough, but if you will build in my honour as many temples as stand in honour of the Lord Brahma and the Lord Shiva, then will I help you."

"And how will you help us, Lord Vishnu?"

"I too am a Lord of Creation and I am the Preserver. I will help you to keep for all the time that is to come in this world everything and every thought you know as good."

So men started to build temples in honour of the Lord Vishnu, and the temples of Brahma were left in the care of the old people. The temples of Shiva were still held in high honour and all the people remembered Kalee.

When the building of many temples had started the people called to Vishnu and said;

"Lord Vishnu, now we have started building many temples in your name!"

"Now I in my turn will help you," Lord Vishnu said. "I will dream my spirit into a boy child and he will live among you and live with you and fight for you and teach you many things. In this way will I help you to keep what you see as good."

"Lord Vishnu, this is a riddle to us. What will these teachings be and how will we know this child?"

The Lord Vishnu replied, "The teachings will be what you will make them to be, and you will know the child in whom my spirit lives by his colour. He will be coloured blue."

And so the world waited for the promise of the Lord Vishnu to become true.

The Blue Boy

Many years after Lord Vishnu had made his promise and when many temples had been built in his name, there lived a wicked king named Kansa. His wickedness came from his father, a gold and scarlet demon who, while flying past the windows of the palace, had seen Kansa's mother asleep on the floor and, swooping into the room on leathery wings, made a child with the beautiful girl while she slept.

Kansa had a sister named Devaki. Devaki was as pure and good as Kansa was wicked and all the young men in the kingdom burned with love for her.

The time came when Devaki chose the man she wished to be the father of her children. This man was Vasudeva, a handsome man who had no liking for Kansa.

"How so bad a man could have so pure a sister I do not know," Vasudeva would say to himself. He did not know of the strange way in which Kansa's mother had come to be with child.

On the day of Devaki's wedding, the whole city lined the streets to watch the procession as it passed between the palace and the temple. Devaki and Vasudeva sat side by side in a great golden carriage drawn by a team of eighteen pure white horses. On the back of each horse, swaying to its movement, sat a coiled and hooded serpent, gilded and with a precious stone set between its eyes. The serpent-mounted horses were driven by Kansa himself, who sat high on a driving seat in front of the happy couple, wearing a long cloak made entirely of peacock plumes held to each other with links of silver thread.

After the ceremony had been blessed and as they returned to the palace, the skies opened above them. A great black voice of thunder, the voice of Indra, spoke to Kansa.

"Kansa, a child of the girl you drive will be your slayer."

Tales of Preservation

Hearing this, Kansa felt terror in his heart. No sooner was the carriage within the palace gates than Kansa leapt to the ground and made towards Devaki, drawing his knife and intending to kill his sister. Vasudeva, who too had heard the voice of Indra, placed himself before his young bride and stayed Kansa's dagger.

"If you spare her life, Kansa, I will bring you each of our children at the moment of their birth," promised Vasudeva. Half-willingly, Kansa agreed, but still he put his sister and her husband in locked apartments with palace guards at the doors every minute of the day and night.

And so the young pair lived with a few companions who had been sent from the palace court. Over the years Devaki bore six little children, each one of which Vasudeva sent to Kansa at the moment of its birth and each one of which Kansa had thrown down the palace well.

"Life is so cruel," Devaki would say to her husband, with great sadness. "When can I bear a child to keep?"

"Soon, Beloved," Vasudeva would say. "The gods will send help to us – I know it."

Devaki fell with child for the seventh time, but this time the gods took the child from her body when it was just the length of a thumbnail and placed it in the womb of one of her palace companions, Rohini. Kansa was told that Devaki had lost her child, and so cared nothing when Rohini bore a little boy she named Belarama.

They had been captive fourteen years when Devaki conceived for the eighth time. Now Kansa dreamt of death. He multiplied the guards around the apartments threefold, and came himself each day to see the increased swelling of his sister's belly.

Tales of Preservation

On the evening that Devaki's eighth child was expected, the gods spoke to Vasudeva.

"Tonight, Devaki will give birth to a son. Take him to the bed of Yasoda, the wife of Nanda the cowherd. Yasoda will also bear a child. Place Devaki's child by the side of Yasoda and bring hers in its place to Devaki."

At midnight, Devaki's child was born.

"His name is Krishna," Devaki told her husband. Vasudeva took the child up, wrapped it in a silken shawl and went into the night. The doors were open although their locks were still tight, the guards were sleeping with open eyes, and all the stars over the palace roofs stood still. Taking one of the great gilded palace serpents from its basket by the stables to guide him through the night, Vasudeva hurried towards Nanda's home.

The river Yamuna was in their path, but as Vasudeva and the snake approached the waters so they receded and dried, leaving a path from bank to bank.

Unseen, Vasudeva reached the hut where Nanda and Yasoda lived. After silently exchanging Krishna for the babe of the sleeping cowgirl, he returned safely to Devaki in her prison.

On his return the doors clanged shut, the guards awoke, and the stars moved through the heavens again. Hearing the cry of a newborn child, Kansa rushed to the apartments and, coming to Devaki's bedside, seized the child she held. Taking it by one leg he started towards the palace well, but at that moment the babe floated free from his grasp and escaped through a great opening in the ceiling, calling out as it soared to the deep blue sky above.

The Blue Boy

"You are a fool, Kansa," the babe cried. "I am Yoganindra, the great illusion, the stuff of dreams. The child who will kill you is born, and he is alive and well."

Kansa felt the hand of the gods and was very frightened. He shut himself up in a single tower at one end of the palace and let no one into his room. But, realising that no more harm could come to him from Vasudeva and Devaki, he set them and all of their companions free.

Vasudeva took Belarama from Rohini and, after promising to make another child with her to take his place, he took the child to join Krishna with Nanda and Yasoda. He bade the cowherd and his cowgirl wife to take the two boys to a place named Gokula, where there was grass and water and many people herding cattle, and where the children could grow together in peace.

Kansa consulted his father, the demon, on the best way of ridding himself of the child who was his enemy. On his advice Kansa ordered the massacre of all young children in his kingdom.

Then started a terrible year in which demons sent by Kansa stalked the land, and many innocent children died. But when the slayers came to the house of Nanda and Yasoda, Belarama hid in the belly of a cow and the gods cut a piece of cloth from the sky and draped it over Krishna, so he could not be seen. The cloth was blue as the sky and in being covered by the cloth, Krishna took up its colour.

It is for this reason that for the rest of his marvellous life his skin was tinged a clear and beautiful blue. And when this was seen men knew the Lord Vishnu had kept his promise and many people came to Gokula to be near to Krishna.

The LoVeS oF QueeN Pritha

The Loves of Queen Pritha

Vasudeva, the father of Krishna, had a sister named Pritha. She had been taken as a young girl into the household of the King of Shuraseva who had his palace high in the Vindya Mountains. Pritha grew into a beautiful doe-eyed girl with a musky fragrance that hung in the air around her and teased the young men as she passed.

One day the wise man Durvasas came to the palace. This was the same Durvasas, one of the seven wise men born of the mind of Brahma, who had cursed Indra before the churning of the Milk Ocean. The King of Shuraseva sent Pritha to attend on Durvasas and for a whole year the young girl served the wise man in the guest quarters of the palace.

When Durvasas left the palace he said to Pritha, "Your sons shall be five in number, and they shall be the sons of gods."

"But how – and what gods?" asked Pritha, startled and puzzled.

"How? Because in return for your kindness in this year past I shall make it so," said Durvasas, "and you may choose the gods yourself."

Tales of Preservation

And Durvasas gave Pritha the words of the charm she should use each of the five times she wished to call a god to her. When he had gone, Pritha returned to her rooms and thought of what the wise man had told her.

"I wonder what it is like to make a child with a god," she mused to herself as she gazed out into the sunlit garden.

"I wonder if the charm Durvasas gave me works?" she thought as she lay down to rest on the floor of her room.

"Surya, Surya, let your spirit fill me so I may have your child," she whispered, drifting gently to sleep.

Summoned by the charm Surya the Sun God appeared in Pritha's room, shining a glowing warm light onto the body of the sleeping girl. In this way he made a child with her.

Pritha woke from her sleep with a great start. Dimly she remembered from her dreams a golden vision and a feeling of great warmth, but that was all. She left her room and went to sit in her usual place by the feet of the King in his council chamber.

Soon Pritha knew the meaning of the dream and in due time, secretly, in the gardens of the palace, gave birth to a boy child whom she called Karna. And, secretly, she made a basket of rushes that she covered with melted wax. Placing the carefully wrapped babe in it she sent the basket gently floating down the river Aswa. As the basket and her first born slipped from view she prayed to Surya, the child's father, and to Varuna the god of all the waters, to keep Karna from harm, and returned sadly to the palace.

The Loves of Queen Pritha

Some months after Pritha had given birth in secret to Karna, the King decided that it was time for Pritha to take a husband. He ordered a great feast to be prepared, lit a fire of ceremony in the main courtyard of his palace and summoned all the kings and princes for miles around to be his guests at Pritha's choosing. With flowers in her hair, a garland in her hand and threads of the finest gold and silver in her clothing, the fragrant and beautiful Pritha moved from prince to king and king to prince as they sat cross-legged on crimson cushions waiting for her to make her choice.

"Him I choose, the pale one, the Bharata," said Pritha, pointing to a king named Pandu. She placed the garland that she carried over the young king's shoulders.

King Pandu's palace was in a great city named Hastinapur that had been built by the first of the Bharata line, a family of great wealth and importance many years before. Pandu's father had been a yogi who had left the palace to live in the woods where he became lean and scrawny with matted locks and smelling of death. When the yogi held Pandu's mother to him to make a child with her, the girl had turned pale at the touch of the old man and so her babe was born pale also.

After Pritha had chosen she left the palace of the King of Shuraseva to travel to Hastinapur with King Pandu. There she met Madri, already a wife of King Pandu and his favourite. Madri, who was dusky as Pandu was pale, had not chosen Pandu as her husband in the way that Pritha had. Madri had been purchased by the uncle of King Pandu in the land of Kashmir, where she lived.

With many chests filled with jewels and with arm and ankle bracelets made in silver and gold, all carried on the backs of elephants and many horses, Pandu's uncle had travelled north to find and purchase Madri. When he had returned to Hastinapur with her she came carried in a chair held aloft by one hundred warriors so all the people could see her and marvel at her beauty.

Pritha and Madri shared everything. They shared the same apartments in the palace; they ate food from the same kitchen; they walked in the same gardens; they shared everything the King gave them. And they shared the King.

They also shared a great sorrow. Much as the King walked in the glades of the forests with them, and much as he played with them in the palace pools filled with the blue flowered lotuses, he made no children with them. He dared not. In his youth he had been told that he would die at the moment he made a child with his wife.

At length Pritha told King Pandu of the charm Durvasas had given to her and, anxious that the line of the Bharatas should be seen to continue, he agreed to her having children by the gods. First Pritha called down Dharma, the God of Justice.

"Dharma, Dharma, let your spirit fill me so I may have your child." As she slept the god Dharma alighted on her pillow and entered her ear, filling her head with wisdom. And in due time, Pritha had a boy child she named Dharmaputra.

Next she called down Vayu the Wind God by invoking the charm, and Vayu sent a breeze that gently ruffled the clothing from Pritha as she lay sleeping. And from her union with Vayu, Pritha produced another boy child she named Bhima.

Then Pritha called on Indra to come to her. Hearing the charm, Indra threw down a thunderbolt as Pritha walked in a forest glade and, as Pritha stood dazed by the noise and light, Indra came down to earth himself and taking Pritha to him made a child with her.

Tales of Preservation

❧ 190 ❧

Pritha, after giving birth to her fourth boy child whom she named Arjuna, resolved to give the charm to Madri who was still childless. Madri was clever as well as beautiful and she wanted more than one child, so when Pritha had given her the charm she called up to the sun; "Surya, Surya, send down your twin sons so that their spirits may fill me and I may have children." Surya sent down his twin sons, the Gods of the Morning, and they came to Madri with laughter and light as she walked amongst the flowers in the gardens, and she gave birth to twin boys whom she named Nakula and Sahadeva. Soon after she had given birth to the twins, King Pandu was so overcome by the beauty of Madri that he forgot the omen of his youth and sought to make a child with her as they sat amongst the grasses of the forest. As he did so the curse came to his mind, but it was too late and in an instant Pandu the pale King of Bharata lay dead. Soon after, the beautiful Madri died also.

The five children of Pritha and Madri became known as the Pandavas and were brought up by Queen Pritha in the palace at Hastinapur with their cousins, the Kauravas, who were the children of King Pandu's blind brother. The Pandavas and the Kauravas grew to hate one another and fought each other through all their lives for the Bharata throne.

How Karna, the first son of Pritha given to her by the Sun God Surya, came to fight on the side of the Kauravas against his brothers and how he was killed by Arjuna is part of another great story. That story came to be known to the whole world, to be told and retold in wonder through all the rest of time.

Rama & Sita

Rama and Sita

When Hanuman was not fighting demons or lashing the sea into foam with his tail or rescuing the poor and helpless, he would go into the mountains to think. High in the peaks he would sit, looking down into the world with wise brown eyes and puckered brow. After many years of thinking, Hanuman had collected together a great store of knowledge and had become very wise. So wise did he become that Sugriva, the King of the Monkeys, who was a son of Surya, the Sun God, and who lived in the Nilgiri Mountains, made Hanuman his chief counsellor. It was in this way that Hanuman started on his last and greatest adventure.

The noble Prince Rama, who was ever mindful of the Lord Vishnu, had come to Sugriva in great distress. Ravana, a fearful ten-headed demon, furious that Rama had spurned the love of his sister, had carried off the Princess Sita, Rama's only and much-loved wife. Far to the south, to the island of Lanka, had Ravana carried Sita and placed her in the care of a horde of demon women to watch over her day and night.

Rama knew only that Ravana had carried Sita southward. Rama had travelled far in his search for Sita and, guided by Vishnu, he had met an elf who was imprisoned in the body of a hideous monster. Rama had freed the elf by killing the monster, and in return the grateful elf had told him that, to overcome the power of Ravana, Rama would need the help of Sugriva and his armies of monkeys.

Sugriva knew of the theft of Sita. Some days before Rama arrived, Sugriva had been walking on a mountain path when a ring made of gold and rubies had fallen onto the rocks beside him. Looking up, he had seen a winged and many-headed demon flying southwards through the clouds and holding to him a struggling princess with long flowing hair. And as he watched them, the princess pulled more rings from her fingers and the bangles from her wrists and let them fall to the earth below. Sugriva collected up all the rings and bangles and gave them to his monkey wives to guard with care.

"These are the jewels of Sita," said Rama, when Sugriva showed the rings and bangles to him. "She dropped them as a sign for me to follow." Rama told Sugriva how Ravana had taken his wife in vengeance, and he asked Sugriva for his help to rescue her. Vishnu put it into the mind of Sugriva to call Hanuman, his chief counsellor.

Hanuman, in his great wisdom, told Sugriva to make a pact with Rama. And the pact was this: if Rama would help Sugriva to slay the evil monkey Bali, who had stolen Sugriva's palace and his throne, then Sugriva would send his monkeys to search for Sita. So Sugriva challenged Bali to a duel and when Bali came down from the mountain where the palace of Sugriva was, Rama took his bow and shot an arrow that felled Bali to the ground and killed him. Then Sugriva, after much rejoicing and merriment at the death of Bali and the return of his palace and his throne, raised four great monkey armies. The army that he sent to the south he put under the charge of Hanuman.

Swiftly Hanuman and his army moved. They searched for signs of Sita as they went.

Rama and Sita

On and on they went, bouncing from rock to rock, leaping through the trees of the forests, peering into caves and under waterfalls and always calling Sita's name. At length they came to the edge of the great Southern Ocean and as far as they could see there was nothing but lines of waves all flaked with foam and rolling in to break on the wide, wild shores.

"Now where do we go?" asked Hanuman's army. Like all monkeys they were frightened of the sea and they sat huddled in misery on the rocks high above the surf, watching the green waters with worried, wrinkled brows.

"You go to Lanka," came a voice. Turning around the monkey army saw they were being watched by an aged vulture who had hopped down to them from the mountains. This vulture had singed his wings from flying too close to the sun and, while waiting for his feathers to mend, he was sitting in the tops of the mountains using his great far-reaching eyes to watch the world. He could see far across the southern ocean and had seen when Ravana had brought Sita to Lanka and hidden her with the demon women in his palace there.

"You go to Lanka and there will you find the Princess Sita," continued the vulture. And he told Hanuman and all his monkey army how far Lanka was across the sea, how great the walls of Ravana's palace were and where he had seen Ravana hide Sita away.

"But how shall we get to Lanka?" asked Hanuman. "We cannot swim."

"But you can jump," replied the vulture.

"Only you can jump that far," said all the monkeys to Hanuman.

So Hanuman climbed to the tops of the mountains in which the vulture had been sitting, grew himself to an enormous size and leapt with a thunderous roar and proudly upheld tail through the skies towards the island of Lanka.

Ravana in his palace felt the distant mountains shake as Hanuman leapt and, looking seaward, saw the gigantic form come hurtling with flashing eyes and the speed of winds towards him. And so Ravana sent his demons to fight with Hanuman and defend the palace. First he sent a giant sea serpent, the mother of all sea serpents, who rose, writhing and scaly, from the depths and opened her mouth so wide that it filled the sky and there was no room for Hanuman to pass. But Hanuman flew straight into the serpent's jaws and nipped out of the side of her mouth just as she closed her jaws with a triumphant snap.

Next Ravana sent the daughter of a dragon who hid in the clouds when evening came and, as Hanuman passed, caught hold of his shadow cast by the last of the sun and pulled him back towards her. Again Hanuman made himself very small and twisting in the air like a whirlwind flew into the demon's mouth and out through her right ear growing large again as he did so, so that she was killed and fell with a gigantic splash into the sea below.

Ravana saw the great bulk of the dragon fall from the sky and, thinking it was Hanuman, left the palace wall. He did not see the cat-like figure that landed on the sandy beach, stealing through the moonlit trees that bordered the shore and, leaping from shadow to shadow, scaled the gates of the palace courtyard and dropped on all fours at the foot of the stairway leading to Ravana's private apartments.

Once inside the palace, Hanuman padded stealthily along the corridors and in and out of room after room. All the treasures of the earth and sea were in the palace.

Rama and Sita

The floors were laid with shells and honey-coloured opal. The walls were hung with curtains woven from the finest filaments of gold and the ceilings were made of crystal quartz in wafers cut so thin that the sun and the moon and the stars shone through them for all to see.

In one room Hanuman found Ravana with his wives. Hidden behind a table near the door, Hanuman watched while the great ten-headed demon lay on a thousand silken cushions and was fed with fruits and fermented juices by the soft-speaking fragrant beauties. Time after time was a golden goblet emptied into the mouths of Ravana until, with his heads in the laps of the most beautiful of his wives, he closed his twenty eyes and slept.

On and on went Hanuman in his search for Sita. He looked in the cupboards, up the ladders, down the wells, through the laundries and the kitchens, behind open-fronted boxes in which bat-headed demons hung upside down on guard, and under tables heaped with mounds of scented blossoms. Finally, Hanuman found his way to the palace gardens and there he spied a grove of trees with lanterns hanging from the branches. Quietly he crept through the flowers and from bush to bush until he reached the trees. Once there, he jumped up into the branches, looked down and saw the Princess Sita surrounded by the fearful demon women. They had the heads of pigs and foxes, with ears kept pricked to catch the slightest sounds. Their eyes glowed red and with their crooked hands they scratched their hairy pot-shaped bellies, which dragged along the ground between their cloven feet.

All night Hanuman crouched in the branches waiting for the chance to speak to Sita. Just before the dawn the horrid demons fell one by one into a snoring sleep. Nimbly

Hanuman jumped to Sita's side and told her of Rama's search for her, and of the army which the monkey King Sugriva had mustered for her rescue. He asked her for a message that he could give to Rama. Taking a jewel from her hair, Sita told Hanuman to give it to Rama with the message that after two more moons Ravana would feed her to the demon women unless she had agreed to be his wife. At this Hanuman grew angry and, growing himself again to a great size, laid about him with his tail. He raised a storm of wind and rain that stripped the leaves from the trees and blew them so hard and in such a fury that they streamed like a swarm of angry bees into the palace and stung Ravana awake from his bed of silken cushions.

"Who raises this storm of leaves?" cried out Ravana, and he sent a band of demons out into the dawn-lit gardens. Fiercely Hanuman and the demons fought each other all through the morning. Sharp-toothed monsters hung from the hair on Hanuman's flanks as he lashed his tail and sent storm clouds tearing through the air. Soon all the trees and flowers were flattened and the ground was heaped with the piles of bruised and bleeding demons. At last Ravana's son came from the palace and fired a magic arrow which wrapped itself round Hanuman from his ankles to his neck so that he fell bound and helpless to the ground.

"Kill him," ordered Ravana, when Hanuman was brought before him. But an elderly demon, his body covered in grey and green mosses, intervened.

"Send him back to whence he came," the demon said, "but first singe every hair from his insolent tail so none will come in his place." And so Ravana had oil-soaked rags wrapped round Hanuman's tail and with an evil grin set fire to it.

"Fly, Hanuman!" cried Sita. Hanuman shrank himself to the size of a girl's finger,

Rama and Sita

slipped from his bonds, raced through the palace with his flaming tail so that it all blazed with fire and, making himself of giant size again, leapt from the shores of Lanka, soared over the sea and rejoined his army where he had left them.

With great rejoicing, Rama and Sugriva prepared to rescue Sita. The monkey army built a chain of islands to bridge the sea to Lanka, and Vishnu sent Varuna, God of the Oceans, to bear the islands up. In five days all was ready and Rama, seated on the shoulders of the faithful Hanuman, led the bouncing chattering horde to confront Ravana and his demon hosts upon the plains of Lanka. For two days the battle raged and after the first day many monkeys and many demons were killed and wounded. But Hanuman leapt into the North and brought back a whole mountain with plants growing on it to heal the monkeys' wounds and bring them back to life again. And so it was that on the second day the monkey army was the same in size and the demon army was diminished.

On the afternoon of the second day Ravana drove out from his palace courtyard in a chariot drawn by wolves to fight with Rama. And Rama drove against him in a chariot drawn by white stallions sent down from the heavens by Indra. Six times they circled each other in their chariots, and six times they fought each other. Then Rama took an arrow blessed by all the gods and, aiming it at the centre of the demon's chest, split him in two so that he lay dead on the plain with five heads looking into the east and five looking to the west. As those demons that remained fled screaming and weeping to hide in the forests of Lanka, the gods let fall a great shower of flower petals to cover the shoulders of Rama and the army of triumphant monkeys.

When Rama had returned to his own country with the Princess Sita he spent many days giving thanks to the Lord Vishnu, and he gave great riches to Sugriva and the generals of his monkey armies.

Turning to Hanuman he said, "And you my faithful friend who found Sita for me, what can I give you?"

Hanuman, looking at Rama with his wise brown eyes, replied, "All I ask is that I may stay in this land for as long as men shall tell the story of Rama and his search for Sita."

And that is how Hanuman's last great adventure ended and why, as we read of Rama and Sita, we can be sure that he sits in the hills and in the trees and in the plains and watches us.

The City of Dwaraka

The City of Dwaraka

All through their childhood Krishna and his brother Belarama lived amongst the cowherds in Gokula. Not knowing where Krishna was to be found, the wicked King Kansa, who sought to kill Krishna, sent his demons to search in every part of the land and kill all children born on the same evening as he.

One evening Krishna was walking amongst the trees near to the home of Nanda when three one-legged demons who were flying through the clouds above saw him and swooped down to follow him quietly along the track below.

When Krishna was deep in the shadiest and greenest part of the wood the first of the demons appeared on the path in front of him. Standing on his one leg, the demon spread his scaly wings, opened his bloody mouth and prepared to swallow Krishna. But Krishna ducked under the gaping jaws, leaned forward and, grasping the demon by his leg, whirled it round and round his head and broke his body like a rotten stick against the trunk of the nearest tree.

Seeing the fate of the first demon, the second turned himself into a huge black crow. Darting forward, with bright eyes fixed on Krishna, he picked him up in his beak and prepared to fly off with him. Krishna made himself grow as hot as a live glowing coal so that the crow's beak began to smoke and he dropped the boy from the pain. Then Krishna leapt upon the crow and standing astride his neck caught hold of his head and twisted it round and round so that the bone snapped and his head turned with the heat-seared beak pointing down at the ground.

On seeing this, the third demon turned himself into a snake that poured and streamed on the ground like melted gold and, on reaching Krishna, opened his fanged mouth and swallowed him whole. Krishna, finding himself suddenly in the steaming heat of the creature's stomach, grew to an enormous size so that he burst through the skin into the world outside leaving the demon writhing to his death besides the remains of his two companions. After this, Kansa sent no more demons to kill Krishna but sent spies to watch him as the blue-skinned boy grew up to manhood.

As Krishna grew so he enjoyed the childhood mischief that exists in all of us. He led Belarama and the other children of the villages to take fruits from the orchards until the old men grew tired of their pranks and scolded Krishna as the cause of trouble. He took water from the river and put it in the milk pails so that the milk would not churn to butter and the milkmaids laboured for nothing. He crept up on cowgirls and stole their clothing as they bathed in the Kalindi River that flowed past the water meadows and then laughed at them in their nakedness. Then, playing on his flute, he crept into the cowgirls' sleep and stole their dreams so that they danced with him in the woods all through the soft warm nights and woke in the mornings with tired legs and heavy-lidded eyes.

The City of Dwaraka

As he grew older, Krishna told all the people of Gokula of the love of Lord Vishnu, the Preserver. He helped them by killing the wicked water snake Kaliya that made the cattle die, and he took up a whole mountain and held it over Gokula to save it from the rain that fell when Indra hurled his thunderbolts.

The spies sent by Kansa told him of all that Krishna did. Kansa, seeking a way to trap Krishna, sent a message to Gokula inviting Krishna and Belarama to come to the city of Muthra and watch a day of wrestling and archery. So Krishna and Belarama tied up their belongings in sacks of jute hung on the end of sticks which they rested on their shoulders and, leaving Nanda and Yasoda and all their cowherd friends in Gokula, set out on the long, hot and dusty road to Muthra. Knowing that the two young men had started on the road, Kansa again sent demons against them. And again Krishna slew them by using his strength and magic powers.

When, after many weeks and many adventures, they reached the gates of Muthra, Krishna and Belarama met an old servant from the palace of Kansa carrying a basket of the King's finest clothes from where he had washed them in the river. Taking the jute sacks from the sticks on their shoulders, Krishna and Belarama threw them upon the old man, one on his head, the other round his feet to tie him and, laying him in the shade of a mule shelter, took the clothes from the basket and strode into the city like two young princes.

All the people of Muthra believed that two sons of a great king from the north had visited the city, but Kansa knew them for who they were by the blue of Krishna's skin. On the day put aside for wrestling and archery, Kansa sent two of his largest and fiercest guards on the back of an elephant to break the bones of Krishna and

Tales of Preservation

Belarama and trample them into the ground. But Krishna, calling on Vishnu to help him, crushed the guards in one of his hands and with the other seized the elephant, held him high over his head and hurled him so that he fell on Kansa and crushed his life from him.

When Kansa's father, the golden and scarlet demon, saw the fearful death of his son he flew screaming to hide far away in a cave in the nether regions. But Krishna rejoiced at the end of his uncle who had brought him so many troubles, and sent for Devaki, his mother and Vasudeva, his father to join him and Belarama in Muthra.

Krishna spent many years bringing peace to the lands around Muthra by killing demons and goblins and other evil creatures. He went on long journeys with Belarama and his army and freed princesses who had been taken captive by wicked kings. Krishna made the princesses his wives and built a walled city by the sea at a place called Dwaraka and lived with them there. Sixteen thousand and eight wives lived with Krishna within the walls of Dwaraka. Krishna proclaimed that Ugrasena who had been King of Muthra before Kansa should also be King of Dwaraka and of all the lands about them.

One day, Arjuna, one of the sons of Queen Pritha, the sister of Vasudeva, came to Krishna at Dwaraka. You will remember that Arjuna and his brothers were called the Pandavas and that there was much hate and trouble between them and their cousins, the Kauravas. Arjuna told Krishna of the wanderings and miseries of the Pandavas who had lost half the kingdom of Bharata.

Krishna befriended Arjuna and told him of the greatness of Vishnu and of how he had guided Rama in his search for Sita. When Arjuna heard of the fall of Ravana on

the plains of Lanka and of the great bravery of Hanuman and all the monkeys sent by Vishnu to help Rama, he asked Krishna how the Lord Vishnu might help him and his brothers in their struggle with the Kauravas.

Krishna listened to Arjuna and said, "I will bring you to the feet of Vishnu just before the last days of your struggle, and just before the day when you will kill your brother."

Arjuna found Krishna's words very puzzling, for he saw no reason to kill any of his brothers who fought beside him against the Kauravas. He did not know that the great warrior Karna, who lived in the court of the Kauravas, had been made by the Sun God Surya with his own mother the Queen Pritha, as the first of her five children.

Arjuna returned to his brothers, taking with him the sister of Krishna to be his second wife. Krishna shared many adventures with the Pandavas in their struggle with the Kauravas. Finally, after the Pandavas had lost the other half of the kingdom of Bharata in a great gambling match and had spent many years wandering in exile, the last days that Krishna had spoken of grew near.

The whole world had known that a final great battle between the Pandavas and the Kauravas must one day take place. Some put themselves on the side of the Kauravas and some on the side of the Pandavas. Those that put themselves on neither side prepared to watch. Krishna went to the Kauravas to search for peace and Queen Pritha told Karna the story of his birth and begged him not to fight his Pandava brothers. But all had been decided by the gods and nothing could prevent the horrors that were to come.

When the first day of the battle came the two huge armies faced one another on a great plain outside the city of Hastinapur. In the front ranks of both armies were rows of chariots. Behind the chariots stood the bowmen, behind them the warriors with swords and spears, and last of all the drummers. Krishna had joined Arjuna in his chariot at the front of the Pandava army to drive his horses. As the dawn broke Krishna kept the promise he had made to Arjuna all those years before and told him of all that he should do to sit at the feet of Vishnu. Everything that Krishna said to Arjuna was heard by those in the army of the Pandavas who were near to Arjuna's chariot and was retold by them on that day and for many days after. The words of Krishna, which came from the mind of the Lord Vishnu, have been heard in every corner of the world from that day on.

For sixteen days and nights the battle raged, and great warriors on both sides fell. On many days Krishna kept Arjuna from harm by his handling of the chariot and his horses. The fighting did not cease at dark, for both armies sought to disturb the sleep of the other and they killed each other in the nights in dreadful ways.

On the seventeenth day of battle Karna and Arjuna met in deadly combat. All through that day they fought, and arrows from both their bows drained dark blood from the wounds of the other. At last the wheels of Karna's chariot became embedded in the muddy battleground and Arjuna, still not knowing that Karna was his brother, shot the life from his helpless enemy with a crescent-headed arrow. Queen Pritha saw the fall of her first born from afar and cried out in pain and grief.

On the eighteenth day the last of the Kaurava brothers died. On the eighteenth night the children of the Pandavas were slaughtered by one of the Kaurava warriors, who then fled with what was left of the Kaurava army. And on the nineteenth day as the Pandavas mourned their children on the field of victory, old Queen Gandhari, mother of the Kauravas, came to look in grief on the torn bodies of her sons. She found Krishna still holding the reins of Arjuna's chariot horses.

"Cursed are you, Krishna," called out the old Queen. "Cursed are you for the aid you gave the enemy of my sons! And as they have died by iron and by arrows so shall you and all your children die."

And with those words in his ears, Krishna left the field of battle and, finding Belarama, rode off to Dwaraka to pass the rest of his days living in peace with his wives.

The Iron Rod

The Iron Rod

I n the city of Dwaraka, Krishna settled to living with his sixteen thousand and eight wives. The land about was peaceful and the crops were plentiful. There were no more demons to be killed and the teachings that had been promised by the Lord Vishnu had been given by Krishna to Arjuna before the battle on the plains of Hastinapur. And so, although he was past his first youth, but not yet nearing the age when his hair would grey and his step would falter, Krishna and his wives made a great many children. One of these children was a boy named Samba.

One day, when Samba was still small and innocent, some twenty of his brothers and sisters strapped a boulder round his middle, placed a veil over his face and took him as a pregnant woman to a yogi, who sat in his orange robes begging alms at a street corner in the town.

"To what child will this woman give birth?" the children asked.

"To an iron rod," the angry sage, who was hungry and not at all deceived, replied. "And it will destroy your father and your father's children and all who walk with him."

Tales of Preservation

The children went away laughing but as the weeks went by Samba began to swell and show all the signs of being with child. This turn of events alarmed all who heard of it and when, in due time, Samba gave birth to an iron rod, the King of Dwaraka ordered it to be ground to power and thrown into the sea.

All of Krishna's children and the children of Belarama, his brother, joined with the people of the city to grind and beat the rod. But try as they might there was one piece that could not be broken, so this fragment – together with the dust that was made from all the rest – was thrown into the sea. In time the iron dust was washed ashore by the ocean's waves and grew into a great bed of steely reeds. A fish that was taken by a fisherman in his nets had swallowed the unbroken piece. The fisherman, finding the iron as he cleaned his catch, took it home to his wife who, seeing the value of a whole belt of cloth in it, told him to sell it to a hunter who lived on the edge of the forest a half-day's walk from them. The hunter in his turn fashioned the piece of iron into the sharp point of an arrow, which he plumed and placed on a shelf to await his next visit to the forest.

The time came when the King of Dwaraka had a fearful dream. In it he saw the walls of the city fall before a great wind, which swept up all the people and blew them like dust across the plains. And then the wind gathered up the people again so that they were lifted and spun round and round, in a spiral that twisted and turned and moved across the land, reaching from the ground and up to the bottom of the clouds. And then the clouds dropped rain and the rain was the people who fell to the ground and broke. When the king looked at the people with their blood soaking into the ground, he saw that each one of them was Krishna.

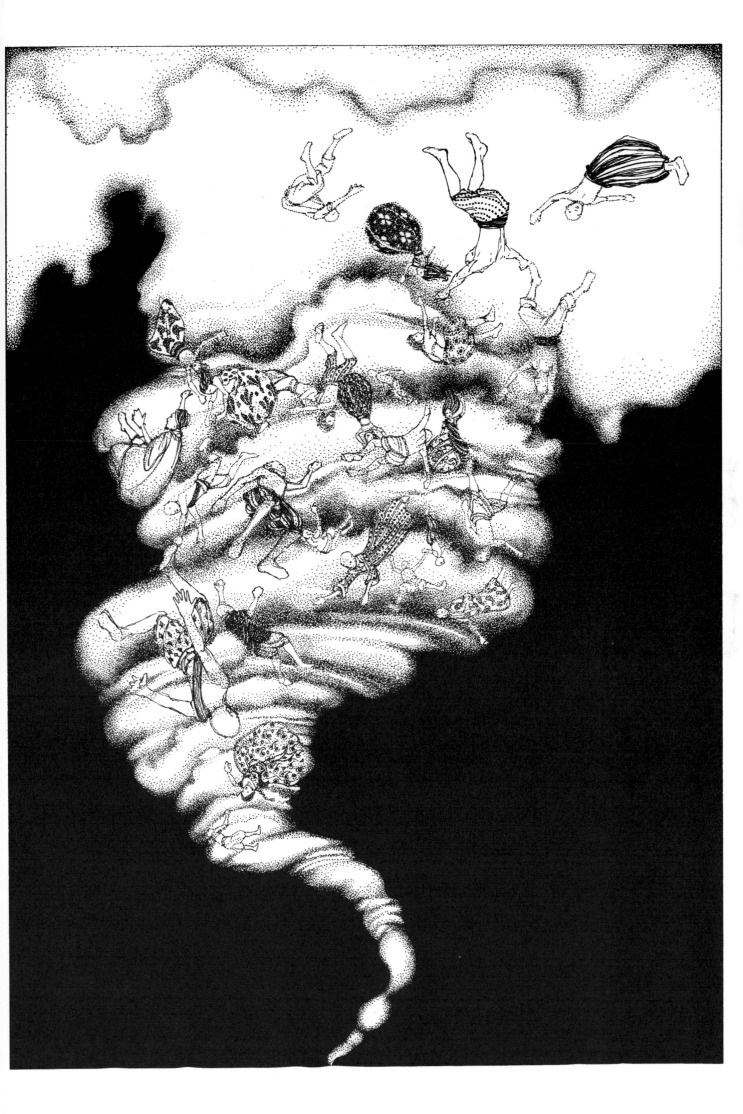

Tales of Preservation

The king went to the temple of Vishnu in the city and told the priests of his dream. On the counsel of the priests, the king went to Krishna to warn him that he and his children were threatened with destruction. Krishna remembered the curse of Queen Gandhari and, calling his wives and his children to him, left the city together with Belarama and the people of Dwaraka. They made their way towards a place called Prebhasa. On the way to Prebhasa they all stopped by the seashore and, making a firing place of stones, unwrapped their stores of lentils, flour and rice and prepared a meal for themselves. Soon a fight broke out between two people as to who should have the first food, and the fighting spread to the many thousands in the group. As they fought, the crowd of people moved across the shore, towards a great bed of reeds. This was the same bed which had grown from the iron dust thrown up from the ocean. Uprooting the hard reeds, the people beat and flogged at each other until of all the thousands who had left the city, only Krishna and Belarama were left alive.

Pressed down with sadness, the two brothers left the pile of battered bodies to be washed and scoured by the sea and made their way along the sand to the forest whose edges reached the shore. There Belarama, overcome by a great tiredness, opened his mouth so that his spirit, which had the form of a golden serpent, slipped out and left him as a lifeless body that lay in the forest's fallen leaves.

Krishna, now completely alone, walked on and sat in the shadow of the trees by the bank of a stream to think of the sorrow in life that had overcome him. The hunter, who that day had come into the forest for the first time in many months, found Krishna and, mistaking him for a deer, shot his life away from him with the iron-tipped arrow.

The Iron Bod

❧

As Krishna's spirit left him the skies, which had lent him their colour so many years before, split open. And all the gods in the heavens and all the creatures in the world and all the demons in the underworld, looked up and saw the Lord Vishnu sitting in the spaces of the universe waiting to welcome Krishna back to him. And from that day men put shrines in their homes and in the temples to honour Krishna as he sits by the side of Vishnu.

Little Gopala

Many years after the death of Krishna and the return of his spirit to Vishnu, an orange-robed yogi came to a village near to where Krishna had lived in Gokula and started to teach the people. Sitting under the peepul tree, which spread its shade at the edge of the village, the old man told of all the teachings of Vishnu that had been spoken to Arjuna by Krishna, and of many other things. In the mornings he taught the children of the village and in the evenings, as smoke from the cooking fires smudged the cooling air, he spoke to their fathers and their mothers.

One morning a poor widow, who had walked a long way into the village to sell butter made from the milk her only cow gave, stopped to listen as the yogi taught the children.

"What fine words," she thought to herself as she trudged slowly through the forest. "I will send my son, Gopala, to sit at the feet of that wise old man." So, when she reached the hut that was home to her and Gopala, she put fresh oil in the lamp that she kept lit in honour of the Lord Vishnu and went to the meadow by the river where Gopala was watching her cow.

"Tomorrow, little cowherd," the widow said, "tomorrow I will watch the cow and you will go to the village to hear the fine words of the yogi."

"But the village is through the forest," said Gopala. "I am afraid."

"You are five years old and too big to be afraid," said his mother.

"Yes," said Gopala, "I am too big to be afraid." But all through the night he thought of the path through the forest and of everything that might hide behind the trunks of the trees.

In the morning he said to his mother, "If a tiger eats me, who then will live in this hut with you?"

"The tiger will not eat you," his mother replied, "for if the tiger comes, you must call to your cowherd brother and he will lead the tiger from you."

"But I have no brother," said Gopala in surprise.

"We all have a brother. Do as I say," said his mother.

So Gopala set off from the village and took the path through the forest. The further he walked from his mother's hut the more certain he was that something followed him.

"It is the tiger," he thought, "and in a minute he will eat me." So shutting his eyes tight he stood by the side of the path and called, "Brother, cowherd brother."

When Gopala opened his eyes he found a boy of his own age standing beside him with a flute in one hand and holding a great tiger on a leash with the other.

"This tiger and I will take you to the village," said the boy. So Gopala and his two companions journeyed through the forest, the boy playing his flute and the great

Little Gopala

tiger growling softly in its throat.

"Go on, go on to the yogi," the boy said to Gopala when they reached the edge of the village. And as Gopala took his place under the peepul tree he looked back to wave to his companions, but there was no sign of them.

"I see you were not eaten by the tiger," said the widow when Gopala came to see her in the meadows in the afternoon.

"No, mother, the tiger walked with me to the village," he replied, and told his mother all that had happened.

"And were you afraid when you walked back through the forest?" his mother asked.

"No, mother," Gopala said and he settled to squeezing the teats of their cow so that it gave the few drops of milk it had made in the day. But that night Gopala thought again of the path through the forest and his fears returned.

"What if my cowherd brother is not there tomorrow?" he wondered to himself.

In the morning Gopala said to his mother, "If a crack in the floor of the forest opened and the cobra comes to strike me, who will milk our cow then?"

And the widow said, "The cobra will not strike you, for if it comes through the floor of the forest, call to your cowherd brother and he will charm it with his flute."

"Are you sure he will be there again?" asked Gopala.

"Do as I say," said his mother.

So on the second day, Gopala set off again from the village and took the path through the forest. Soon he could hear the rustle of dry leaves and a thousand cobras coming.

"Brother, cowherd brother," he called out. When he opened his eyes there was the boy again and he was playing his flute to a great golden snake that reared and swayed with spreading hood in front of him.

"Kadru, the mother of all cobras, will go with us as I take you to the village," said the boy. Again Gopala and his two companions travelled through the forest to the village, the boy playing his flute and the snake pouring through the grasses like a stream of whispering gold. And again when Gopala turned to wave, the boy and the creature had vanished.

"The cobra did not come then?" asked his mother.

"Yes, it did," said Gopala, and he told his mother of the beauty of the great snake and how it danced to the tune his cowherd brother played.

And so day after day Gopala walked through the forest to the village and on each day he had walking with him his cowherd brother and a companion from the wild. Soon Gopala knew all the creatures of the forest. He knew the bear and the fox, the wolf and the boar, the thrush and the lizard, the deer and the mongoose. On one day the lowly scorpion scuttled crab-like along the path to the village. Always the cowherd boy walked with him playing his flute.

A morning came when the yogi told the children of the village that on the next day they should bring small gifts of food so that they could make a festival to remember the birthday of Krishna. Gopala went to the meadows where the widow was watching the cow and told her of what the yogi had said.

"When you walk through the forest tomorrow," said his mother, "call to your cowherd brother and ask him for a jar of milk."

"Could I not take milk from our cow?" asked Gopala.

"Our cow is nearly dry," his mother answered. "Do as I say."

So the next day when Gopala was in the middle of the forest, he stood by the edge of the path, shut his eyes tight and called, "Cowherd brother, cowherd brother. Bring milk to me."

When he opened his eyes there was the boy with his flute in one hand and a jar of milk in the other. But it was a jar so small that it would not have capped the top of Gopala's thumb. This time as they walked together the rest of the way to the village Gopala could hear the lowing of a thousand cows so loudly that it nearly drowned the sound of his companion's flute.

"With all those cows, he could have spared me a little more milk," thought Gopala.

When the time came to give the food to the yogi so that he could make a festival, the children stood in a line and Gopala was the last of all. When the yogi saw the size of the jar Gopala carried, he laughed.

"Small measure from a small boy," he said, "but no matter; Krishna was small once."

He took the jar and poured the milk from it into a pan behind him. As long he held the jar opened so the milk poured from it until the pan was filled. Then the yogi called for another pan and that was filled also. Then the yogi looked inside the jar in wonder and when he tilted the jar again, the milk poured from it. Gopala remembered his thoughts when he had heard the lowing of all those cows and the tips of his ears went hot with shame.

"From where did this jar come?" asked the yogi.

"From my brother, my cowherd brother," said Gopala, and he told the yogi of all that had happened to him in the forest and of all that he had seen.

Little Gopala

"I would like to see your brother," said the yogi. So Gopala took the old man by the hand and together they walked into the forest.

"Who told you of your brother?" asked the yogi when they were deep into the trees.

"My mother," said Gopala. "She says we all have a brother. I will call him to you."

Shutting his eyes tight he called out, "Brother, cowherd brother," and when he opened his eyes the boy was there.

"There is my brother," said Gopala to the yogi.

"I see nothing but the sunlight and the shadows," said the old man.

"And listen to the music of his flute," said Gopala.

"I hear nothing but the wind in the trees," the yogi said. Then, looking at Gopala's shining face, he asked, "What is the colour of your brother?"

Gopala answered, "He is the colour of the sky. He is the most beautiful shining blue."

Then the old yogi put his hand on Gopala's head and said, "Go home to your mother and help her with her cow. Come to me under the peepul tree no more."

"But my mother said I should come to hear your fine words," said Gopala.

"My little Gopala," said the old man, "you have five years and I have some five and eighty years but already you have more than ever I can give you. You have no need of fine words."

Gopala went home to his mother and found their cow was giving milk again. The old yogi left the village to travel through the world and tell the story of little Gopala and his cowherd brother who came to him in the forest.

The End

The End

Through all the ages of this world the minds of Brahma the Creator, Vishnu the Preserver and Shiva the Destroyer think and dream. And from their dreams come all the things that are, and all the things that happen, in the heavens and in the world and in the underworld. From those dreams come all these stories, and all the stories that have ever been, and all the stories that are not yet told.

In the world, men call these lords of creation The Great Gods and they honour them. Mankind honours also the other, smaller gods and all the spirits from the heavens, and seeks their help to keep the demons shut tight within the underworld. Especially, men honour the Lord Vishnu for the balance he keeps between the works of Brahma and the works of Shiva, and they remember the teachings that Krishna gave to Arjuna.

If you want to remember how it all began, stand outside on a clear night and look for the stars, which are the beautiful maidens that danced their way to Indra's palace. Stand beside the farthest star you can see, and then look up once more and again set yourself beside the farthest star you can see. Do this three times, then close your eyes and open your ears. Then will you hear the mighty sound of Aum as it roars through the silence that is everywhere.

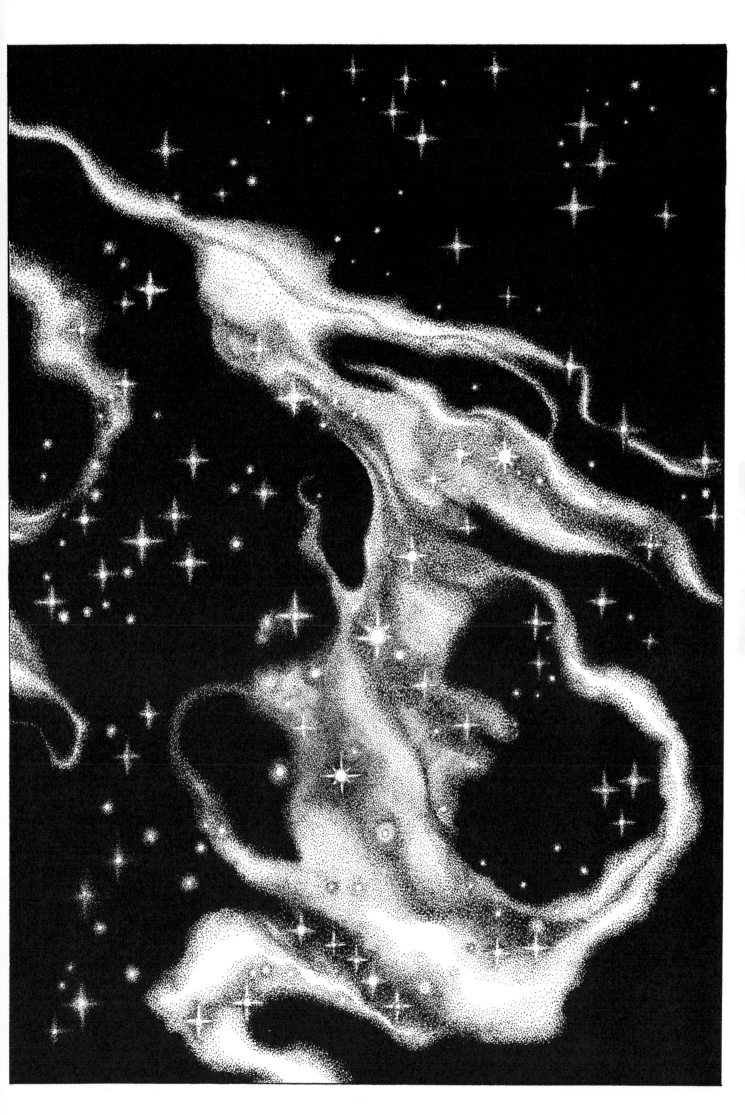